Cactus Country

**Center Point
Large Print**

ॐ श्री गणेशाय नमः

Cactus Country

Lauran Paine

Center Point Publishing
Thorndike, Maine

CONTENTS

ONE

AT DAY'S END

Westerly, the sun touched the farthest mountains and seemed to be pierced by a high peak, because there was a dazzling burst of red which coloured the spires and hillocks and rough-cut rimrocks with dying day's last shades of rusty-red.

Dozens of separate prisms of light flashed along both sides of the dusked canyons, and out across the springtime desert an aurora which was shaped to the pitch and curve of the farthest earth held time still in its tracks for as long as was required for heaven and earth to merge in their faded pastels, then it all began to crumple.

Twilight came out of the far mountain canyons, bone-dry blueness trickling from the far-away foothills out across the cactus country, inundating it.

A desert evening was hauntingly spectacular any time of year, but in springtime the desert was best in *all* ways.

The laughter of a woman rising against the fluted columns of oncoming night, the ring of spurs along with the rattle of rein-chains, and shod hooves grating over abrasive desert chat, equalled the cellos of elsewhere, and the plumbless depths of silence yonder below the town of Duro where the desert ran full-length to the Mexican border and far beyond, down into the Provinces of Chihuahua and Sonora, was what made those sounds so precious to men.

The peculiar silence of the seemingly endless desert was part of the entire unique montage of an earth-segment unique to the Southwest. It was the same silence that kept vigil over lost graves from west Texas to southern California. The same hush that haunted men who were accustomed to sound and drove them out of their hiding places into the border towns of New Mexico and Arizona. It was the brimstone soundlessness of the grave, and it accomplished something noise never did, it played upon the thoughts, but mostly upon the consciences, of men.

Silence could do that, noise couldn't.

As the sturdy man leaning upon the paloverde fence said to the girl with the taffy hair and the gunmetal eyes, "You don't work at adjusting to it; you can't work at making yourself like something this big and overwhelming and changeless, and if you try, it'll get you the same way it gets those men who come out of it every now and then as crazy as a pet 'coon. You accept it." The man turned and smiled, his bronzed face lined but youthful. "Sure, you can learn about it, but don't make yourself like it—or dislike it. Look; there is it, thousands of miles of it, a real man-killer if a person makes it that way." He reached for her cool hand, turned and slow-paced back up the evening-cool springtime dusty wide roadway. "Don't worry about it one way or another. You're *here*, it's *there*," he shrugged powerful shoulders.

She said nothing. They walked quietly through the empty night. She had met him only the day before, but he was so easy to be with it was almost as though she had known him for years. Nor did she pull her hand away from him; that, too, seemed very natural.

At the wide, low steps leading to the church, she turned in, found a place and sat down, drawing her knees up a little to be encircled by her arms. She was a tall girl, leggy and small-breasted and lean-flanked, actually boyish with her short, curly, taffy hair, but no man would ever have mistaken her for anything but a woman. In all the ways that counted, she *was* a woman. When she tilted her face to gaze up at him, her mouth was wide and ripe, her throat showed a quick pulse, and the gunmetal eyes reflected a soft-sad expression that mirrored both trust and acceptance.

Her name was Joyce Kincaid. She wasn't a city-girl even though the bronzed man acted towards her as though she were. In fact, she had been born and raised at army posts along the edge of Indian country all the way from Commancheria to Fort Apache, but Duro had no army post and very little else that reminded her of the environment she had matured in; no dawn-bugles, no dusty parade ground, no "laundry-row" where fascinating scraps of gossip were available to those who listened, and no lean-flanked booted, sweat-streaked troopers who always smelled of horse-sweat, sage and sand and tobacco.

She smiled upwards. "I know the desert country. The only time I was away from it was the summer before the Flint Hills Massacre. And afterwards, I came back to it."

He stood hip-shot watching her, the gloves shoved under the front of his gun-belt of soft doeskin, the boots he wore scratched and scarred, and the big-row-elled spurs slathered over with silver which had been beautifully chased and engraved, in the Spanish and Mexican style.

He could have been any kind of a Southwesterner; a rangerider, a stage-driver, a lawman even, or an outlaw. He was no better than average in height, but his body was compact, powerful, with strength and muscle packed beneath a sun-blasted hide. He was one of those men who never had to prove anything; when his kind appeared in a saloon and even among strangers, he was left strictly alone. Not all men in the cactus country had his calm appearance of total capability, but the best ones had it; the ones who lived longest had it.

"It's been three years," he said to her, then smiled. "I reckon on warm nights like this memories crowd in. I know how that is."

She kept gazing up at him, her own faint melancholy fading somewhat before her curiosity about him. All she knew was what her uncle, John Stedman who owned the general store in Duro, had told her, and that wasn't much. His name was Jefferson Stuart and there was a border-rumour that he had been one of those raiders under General Jubal Early who had burned towns up in Pennsylvania during the war, and for whom federal warrants were still extant, Jubal Early and his chief lieutenants having been excluded from the General Amnesty.

Otherwise, he existed by buying and selling livestock. Around Duro, where the spidery brands of old Mexico mingled with the heavier, less imaginative brands of Arizona, anyone who got a bill-of-sale along with their purchased horse, could be cynically sceptical; horse-stealing had been flourishing for so many generations in the desert country, that even the law accepted it as endemic and traditional. But her uncle had never said Jeff Stuart dealt in stolen animals. In fact, her uncle had said of all the border-types, meaning those who spoke both English and Mex and who belonged in the cactus country, Jeff Stuart was one of the most respected and reliable.

But to a woman there had to be much more to a man than simply these basic things; they bridged a gulf of blurred years and touched upon no details. Women needed to know more.

She said, "You know why I'm here. After

Flint Hills only my mother's uncle was left. He asked me to come live in Duro, and I did. There was no other place for me to go. Why are you here?"

His gaze drifted to the askew wooden cross atop the mud-walled old church, then ranged out and around the dusty plaza of Mex-town before returning to her lifted face. In a quiet, mocking tone he said, "It's been so long now I've half-forgot. Maybe because I like the desert. Maybe because Duro is a peaceful place. Maybe because . . ." He paused. "Maybe because if you have an inner voice, and you listen to it, and it tells you to stay, that's what you do." He held out a hand. She accepted it, allowed him to pull her back up to her feet, then fell in beside him as they strolled back down through the soft-hushed springtime night in the direction of that other part of Duro, the part created by the most recent con-querors of the desert-Southwest where

Main Street had no Mexican names, where the buildings, although still of adobe, because there was no nearby source of lumber, were nevertheless totally different. Mex-town and Yanqui-town backed up to one another, each different, each unwilling to accept too much of the other way of life. Main Street more nearly approximated the cow-town roadways of the more northward country. Mex-town was typical of the more ancient mode of desert existence. The people mingled, but not very compatibly nor comfortably, as a general rule, but they nevertheless coexisted.

In a place where the land was hostile, in order to survive human beings had to rely upon one another.

As they turned out of Mex-town a young man softly playing a guitar somewhere among the adobe *jacals*, his song sad-sounding in the night, made her pause and half turn back.

"What is he saying?"

Stuart watched her profile in the star-hung night. "It's a song about a young man who lives with regret."

Joyce turned. "A love song?"

He nodded.

"What does he regret?"

"She died before he could tell her how much he loved her."

". . . Are they always so sad?"

Jeff smiled, took her hand and gently tugged her along. "Usually, yes. When a Mex sings a happy song he's drunk or else, if he's not drunk, the last line of the song will have a sad or bitter twist to it."

She leaned a little, brushing him at hip and shoulder as they stepped up onto the scuffed plankwalk, heading northward up Main Street in the direction of her uncle's store. "They are a sad people," she murmured, very conscious of him at her side.

He answered with a little grin. "They

have reason to be. This isn't Mexico, and really never was although Mexico used to own it. They've been made slaves by everyone who rode through. Those who didn't want them as slaves, the Apaches for instance, simply killed them. And now we're here. We don't enslave them, we simply turn our backs on them." Stuart jutted his jaw. "See that saloon across the road; just inside the door there's a sign. 'No dogs and no greasers'." He strolled onward, still holding her hand.

"But they are friendly," she said. "I've met them in the months I've been down here, they smile."

"Sure. Like a dog grins at you—hoping you won't kick it."

When they halted out front of the store building, she pulled him around facing her. "You like them, don't you?"

"Yeah, I like them. Most of them anyway."

"Because you speak Mexican?"

He laughed at her. "No. I also speak English, but there's an awful lot of Americans I don't like." He leaned past to try the door, which was unlocked. He shoved it open then stepped clear. "I'm glad I met you down there at the lower end of town tonight. Do you do that very often—go walking in the evening?"

"On nights like this I do," she said, and felt behind her for the doorknob. "I'm glad we met too. Good night."

"Good night."

TWO

A GIRL WHO IS A WOMAN

A successful tradesman who also happens to be a widower, as John Stedman was, quite often becomes, as Stedman had become, so engulfed in business that other things go either unnoticed or unheeded. But having brought his niece to Duro to live with him until she could pick up the strands of her life after losing both parents at the Flint Hills Massacre, up in the Dakotas, John Stedman had those other things, the ones he had been overlooking or side-stepping for many years, brought squarely up to his attention. For example, although he had known Jefferson Stuart for years—he thought it had to be perhaps six or eight years but wasn't certain—he had not formed anything stronger than an acquaintanceship with Stuart, even though they had been meeting in Stedman's big old barn of a general store almost weekly during that rather lengthy time, so, when Joyce would ask questions out of the blue, her thick-bodied, big, greying uncle would peer over the steel rims of his spectacles, at a loss for specific answers.

It was the morning following that meeting southward, where she'd been leaning upon the paloverde fence and Jeff Stuart had walked out to lean there with her, that she wanted more details about Stuart, and her uncle could not give them.

They were working alone in the store piling new bolts of printed gingham upon the dry-goods shelves. She told her uncle of that chance meeting at the lower end of town, then she said, "He was so natural, so pleasant. It was so easy being there talking to him, Uncle John. He's not like the other people I've met here in Duro. When I told

him how mother and father were killed at
Flint Hills, he didn't say how sorry he was,
or how terrible it must have been for me.
He just told me that no matter how bad
violence is, it's nice for people to realise
that what comes after it just has to be so
much better. Did you ever have anyone say
something like that to you?"

John Stedman was a solid six-footer
whose wife had died nine years earlier. He
was in the neighbourhood of his mid-for-
ties, had never had children, and had been
dedicated to his store for almost a quarter
of a century. People did not say things like
that to him; in fact people rarely mentioned anything to John Stedman that did
not have something to do with business.
He was that kind of a man.

He said, "No," with a dubious drag to
his tone. "And I'm not sure what he meant
by that, either."

Joyce turned to watch the square jaw,

the strong, straight-lipped mouth as her uncle boosted a bolt of cloth, then she turned away and also went to work. "I thought he probably meant that no matter how bad life is, death is so much better you'll forget having lived."

This time John Stedman turned his head. He was not a loquacious man, but neither was he totally lacking in humour. He showed an ironic twinkle now, facing his long-legged, handsome niece. "Not many men in this country do that kind of thinking, Joyce. Maybe you're attributing something to Stuart that he doesn't possess."

She swung. "What doesn't he possess, Uncle John?"

They gazed at one another for a moment. John Stedman finally shifted stance and reached for the next bolt of gingham. A man did not have to have raised daughters to sense quick, candid antagonism in a girl. He picked up the cloth before deciding his niece was not being just accidentally defensive. As he boosted the bolt upwards he retreated by saying, "I don't rightly know; all I meant was that Jeff Stuart—well—he's a desert man, and all the desert men I've known in my lifetime, have been hard and tough and very practical people."

She remained defensive. "He could be practical and philosophical too, couldn't he?"

Stedman sighed under his breath. Having this spirited girl around was hard on his settled, ingrown way of life. After a man had developed habits that suited him, well into middle life, he did not particularly enjoy having someone come along who abrasively intruded. But he was fond of her. Her mother had been his only sister and he had been fond of her mother too. She reminded him of her mother in many ways, although she had that leggy, lean, greyhound-build of her father.

They stacked the last bolt of goods. She climbed down from the low ladder and said, "Tell me, honestly, Uncle John; don't you like Jeff Stuart?"

He protested. "Why yes, of course I like him. I told you—he's reliable and folks respect him, which is a very high commendation in this country. I just don't know him very well, and, after all, you are my responsibility." John Stedman smiled a little. "It's reached me late in life, Joyce, and I know very well you're not a small girl in need of protection—but still and all . . ." He turned away to hide his discomfort. He had never in his life spoken to a girl like this before. It made him uncomfortable.

She suddenly swept in close, stood on her toes and kissed him on the cheek. Then she whirled, lifted the little ladder and took it along to the hardware counter where it belonged, and over there, she got very busy with the feather duster.

Morning was the traditional time of day for shoppers to be abroad on the desert, even though in springtime the days did not get as breathlessly hot as they would become later on, in mid summer and autumn.

Stedman's store was the only general store for many miles, it did a very good business, and when the stockmen who operated to the north where the grasslands and hill-country merged with the south-ward desert, sent their wagons down for supplies, Joyce's uncle had to work out back upon his loading dock like a common labourer. But he was accustomed to that.

Also, because Duro was mid-way between the grasslands and the lower desert—and beyond it something like thirty miles, the Mexican border—strangers were commonplace. Hardly a day

passed that weathered, soiled, trail-stained
men did not come in for cartridges and
flour, tobacco and perhaps some rare
luxury like tinned peaches, smile at Joyce
then walk out the door and never come
into her life again.

The U.S. Marshal—actually a *deputy*
U.S. marshal, but no one called him a
deputy—who had an office between the
town-marshal's jailhouse and the gunshop
of an older man named Henry Steele, had
told Joyce shortly after her arrival in Duro,
that perhaps a half of the men she sold
tobacco and flour to, were fugitives riding
hard for the border. When she had asked
why, if he knew this, he did not arrest
them, Marshal Hyatt Sumner gave a practical answer.

"If a man robs a stage a hundred miles
north or east of here, and rides hard, he
can be in Duro the next day on his way
over the line, and the post carrying his

description and crime won't get down here for three, four days. Now then, if I corraled everyone I didn't like the looks of, and jugged them until the mail came, even if half of 'em were fugitives, the other half would raise hell and prop it up, and I'd lose my job wouldn't I?"

Hyatt Sumner had laughed at Joyce's expression. He was a man almost as old as her uncle, but thinner and more sinewy in his rangy, lanky way. "You just go on selling them ammunition, trying to guess which ones are outlaws, and I'll just go on doing like I've always done—catch the ones I can, and sit here waiting for the other ones to get homesick and risk riding back up through out of Mexico."

Hyatt Sumner was, in a different way, a little like Jeff Stuart in his outlook. Stuart seemed more tolerant. Marshal Sumner seemed more patient. One might overlook something, the other one would *seem* to overlook it, but actually he would only be waiting for his chance to do something about it.

The morning after her pleasant, twilight walk with Jeff Stuart, with her thoughts still very much on him, when Henry Steele the gunsmith ambled in for a plug of Horseshoe chewing tobacco, he gave her an even more definite explanation of the difference between those two men. When she mentioned them old Steele, digging in his accordion purse for the coin to buy his plug, said, "One lost, the other won." He put down the coin and raised his wise, faded eyes. "One was with the Union. That was Hyatt Sumner. He was a cavalry officer. Them fellers won. Jeff Stuart was a Confederate, a Secesh, and they lost, and fellers as lose got to be more tolerant, don't they?"

She watched the gunsmith amble back out of the store. These men were different from the types she had known at those army posts where she had grown up. They saw the same things from a different plateau. It would be many years before Joyce Kincaid would understand why there was this difference, and which aspects of it might be more nearly pragmatically correct than the other aspects.

Along towards late morning when the customers thinned down to a few who, invariably, could not make up their minds, her uncle came along to say he'd be out of the store for a bit.

This was something he had developed since she'd arrived to clerk in the store. He hadn't been able to leave during working hours before; not since his wife had died almost ten years previous. He went over to Murphy's Sahuaro Saloon and drank a cool beer. It had become part of his daily routine, these past few months. He looked forward to it every morning, and Joyce thought it was probably a very good thing for her uncle to do. He met men over there which he otherwise only met across a store-counter. It was a good thing for him to get clear of the store for a while.

She finally satisfied her last customer, a small, dark, nervous woman who was trying to match cloth to thread, and was putting the rejected spools back into their little glass-fronted case when she heard—and recognised—the spurs at the roadway door. She looked around.

He ambled in smiling, his stiff-brimmed, low-crowned borderman's hat shoved back to show slightly curly, coarse-textured sandy hair.

She smiled back. "I knew who it was before you came in."

He nodded. "Sure. Have you ever noticed on a cow outfit how the dogs can tell who's coming the same way you knew it was me?"

She had had no experience on ranches; the only cowmen she'd associated with had been irate ones who had come to the posts to denounce the army for not preventing holdouts and stronghearts from killing and stealing their cattle. But she understood what he meant. "Do all spurs ring differently, then?"

He leaned upon the counter gazing past out into the sunbright roadway. "I reckon. Not to me, but dogs can sure tell, and some folks can. Me, I know a Chihuahua from a California spur when they ring, but it's got to be that big a difference." He shifted his attention back to her. "I'm going down over the line. I was thinking this morning that I'd like to bring you something back. But you don't wear jewellery, do you?"

She didn't; at least she very rarely wore jewellery. But what came over her now was a hint of faint discomfort; a man bringing gifts to a woman implied something. She finished with the spools, then, without looking at him, she said, "I don't want anything." She still did not look at him, but she sensed a change between them and was tempted to raise her face from the thread-cupboard.

He was silent for a time, until he straightened up off the counter. "Well; it was only a thought." He was looking at her profile as he spoke. "I'll—well—I'll be back in a few days."

She looked up, then. "Have a good trip and be careful." She smiled, wanting to say more but feeling unsure of which words to use.

He nodded. "Yes'm."

She watched him return to the roadway wishing she could have thought of something else to say. By the time her uncle returned from across the road she was in an unhappy, quiet mood, something her uncle noticed, and he did not press her at all. He had no idea why women's moods came and went like summer showers; he had never been able to fathom that even when his wife had been alive, but he *had,* as many other men also had, learned that when these things happened, the best course was to stay away, to keep quiet, to become busy elsewhere and when the mood passed, as they invariably did, not to ask questions, but simply be glad it was over.

But it had been a long time for John Stedman. He went to his office, sank down at the desk, hoisted his feet and stared thoughtfully at the fading oil portrait of his wife; in some ways, having his niece around was like having his wife back again. In time, he supposed, he would make the re-adjustment, but a man in his middle forties wouldn't be able to do it as easily as he'd once been able to.

THREE

DOWN THE SILENT WASTE

When there was a moon the desert glowed in springtime with a completely unearthly radiance, and under this aegis, the peculiar, pungent fragrances lingered well past sundown. In the old days deadly little bandy-legged, thick-shouldered, top-heavy Apaches had crept to the edges of settlements to shoot people by moonlight, despite the assurances of later-day "authorities" that Indians did not wage war at night.

But that had been a long while back. Henry Steele remembered, along with a few others, but generally, even men as old as John Stedman and Hyatt Sumner, had never actually seen a desert raider in the wild, although Hyatt at least had been on chases as a young man. But the trouble had been, back in those days twenty years and more earlier, that pursuing Apaches and catching sight of them were two different things.

But as Hyatt stood now in the dripping dark shadows of the lower end of Duro, evidently waiting, he gazed southeastward where those marauders had once materialised like copper demons, and relaxed against the dark, cool, rough wall of an old roofless, abandoned *jacal*, smoking a cigarette as though, except for wanting not to be seen, he had no worries in the world.

Eventually the light footfall accompanied by a ring of rowel against spur shank arrived, and Marshal Hyatt Sumner dropped his smoke, ground it out, turned and stepped around the ghostly old hutment into the still darker alleyway.

The oncoming man was an inch or two shorter, but thicker from the waist up, more oaken appearing and younger. His face, partially hatbrim-shadowed, partially obscured by alley-gloom, seemed no younger than Hyatt Sumner looked to be in this pitchblende night where moonlight could not reach, but actually Jeff Stuart was easily fifteen years younger than Marshal Sumner; possibly even twenty years younger.

He showed white teeth in a thin smile as the marshal beckoned him over where the darkness was solid. "No one's around," Stuart said softly, "especially at this end of town. The Mexicans turn in when the sun leaves."

Marshal Sumner ignored the comment to say, "Are you all set?"

"Packed and ready," replied Stuart. "You're sure the *Rurales* know; I'd hate like hell to get intercepted down there with what's in my saddlebags."

"They know," Sumner replied. "Pablo Herrera has your description, and the description of your horse and outfit. Remember what I told you night before last—they aren't going to show up until you've got beyond the village." Sumner drew something from a pocket and handed it over. "Herrera will ask you for this."

Stuart opened his palm, upwards. The small badge showing dully in the darkness. He closed his fingers and pocketed the thing as he dryly said, "Well, I hope to hell Captain Herrera is the only one who sees it, Hyatt. A lot of men have had their hearts blown out from behind, just for carrying one of those things."

Marshal Sumner did not comment. He knew better than Jeff Stuart how true that was. He offered a hand. They shook briefly, solidly, then Stuart turned and went back up the alleyway making scarcely any sound, and U.S. Deputy Marshal Sumner rolled another cigarette, lit it inside his hat, and eventually, after a suitable lapse of time, strolled around in the opposite direction, encountered the eerie, brilliant moonlight, crossed the lower end of Main Street to continue his walk as far as the plaza over in Mex-town where an ancient well in the centre of the broad roadway had been bricked up to slightly more than knee-height. Here, for more generations than anyone could recall, the original dwellers of Duro had been drawing water, bathing babies, doing laundry and simply gossiping, and here, Marshal Sumner stepped up and sat down upon the broad brick wall, still thoughtfully smoking.

Jeff Stuart, meanwhile, had returned to his *casa*, his old Mexican house, near the upper end of Main Street, where he entered the barn and made certain everything was ready for the trip, before ambling on through and going over to the network of faggot-corrals to lean and think, and savour the horse-scent beneath that same old copper-tinted ancient moon.

Stuart's house had once belonged to the *alcaldes,* the mayors, of Duro. He had bought it cheaply from a wispy descendant of the last *alcalde* years ago. It was a delightful home, better than any in Mextown and as good as anything the newcomers had built for themselves to live in. It also had its own well, and a wonderful old patio where a fig tree, an orange tree, and a lemon tree grew—not well, unless Jeff brought plenty of ground pulp from his corrals to nourish them, because the desert's soil was flinty, stingy, and alkaline.

He had neglected to mention his house to Joyce Kincaid as one of the reasons why he remained at Duro. But he had done that purposefully. His reason for this omission was his own. As he leaned there now, in the bland night, he thought of that reason.

Through the tumult of a man's fierce youth he yearned for a woman's soft shoulders the way men in the cactus country yearned for cool water—to relieve a longing, and that was all. For most men the tumult of youth only lasted perhaps a few years; for men hardened in war it lasted longer, and when the echoes diminished and ultimately faded, what a man wanted was still soft shoulders, but he yearned for a whole lot more as well, because he was no longer a youth. He had come from the crucible tempered for deeper thoughts and yearnings.

Someday, Jefferson Stuart might bring the long-legged taffy-haired girl to his *casa*. Someday he would find the woman who would step through the ancient wooden gate and blend perfectly. Someday, sometime, some woman.

He turned, studied the muscular seal-brown horse drowsing near the manger of his corral, saw the glisten of moonglow off a sleek hide, smiled and walked away.

At the house he removed saddlebags from a hollow place beneath the tiled floor, changed his clothes with those saddlebags within reach at all times, heaved them over his shoulder as he went to the kitchen to wrap three warm tortillas in a length of cotton, fill a canvas-wrapped canteen from the bucket on the sink, and, still wearing the saddlebags, leave the house to cross his fragrant patio and step forth through the old carved wooden gate.

The night was waiting.

An advantage to living near the upper end of Duro was that a man could ride out westerly in dark attire, upon a seal-brown horse and, providing he waited until near midnight, he would not be seen at all. Not even any dogs barked.

It was a pleasant night, and on the morrow it would probably also be a pleasant day, even though the name of the town, which had been adapted from what the old ones, *el viejos,* had called the entire countryside, *duro,* meaning hard and cruel and savage and oppressive, certainly did not make a man expect anything benign when he headed down into the desert.

Stuart's powerful horse took the desert in stride, with full confidence in the man upon his back. They had both been down through here many times before, and while in mid-summer, it had been unpleasant, often hellish to make this same crossing, they had always made it, and fortunately, the memory of a horse is very short. Further, the seal-brown had not been out in months. Stuart had ridden other horses, of which he had several corraled and many more wandering loose—but branded— upon some north-country grasslands he owned.

Of them all, the seal-brown was best on the desert. He was not a young horse; desert-men rarely used colts. He was not flighty not easily upset nor excitable, so, without having any idea that it was so, the seal-brown gelding had the ideal temperament for his environment.

They left Duro far back, and encountered a pair of little fragile Swift-foxes hunting together for rodents not far from a fresh turned burrow of moist earth where they probably had a litter, but otherwise there was nothing, not even snakes; the land drowsed on all sides beneath that high and dusty ancient moon.

The seal-brown walked steadily along, reins swinging. Stuart checked his Winchester then shoved it back into the saddle-boot, and for lack of anything else to do, he lifted out the blue-steel Colt and examined it too, which the gun did not need; a man who lived as Stuart lived, had only the four legs beneath him and the six bullets on his thigh as life insurance. If he hoped to continue to survive he was very solicitous concerning both. Especially down along the border where heat and thirst and tick-fever were of dwindling importance as foremost perils the closer one got to the mythical line running mostly east and west, interspersed at intervals by low cairns of whitewashed stones.

There was, probably, more law along the border than there was north or south of it. There was the U.S. army, and over the line, Mexican route-armies. There were always skulking U.S. marshals, and over the line those very deadly little *Rurale* bands of Mexico's constabulary police. There were also, more often than not, incognito lawmen from Texas, Arizona, New Mexico, and California, hunting for some outlaw, and all that law guaranteed trouble for solitary horsemen—unless he could avoid them—and it quite often guaranteed killings. The *Rurales* were brutal men, and fierce as well. But north of the line fast guns and hair-triggers were just as blind-deadly.

The closer a lone horseman got to that imaginary line the greater grew his chances of not living to cross it, or, if he *did* cross it, of not living long after he crossed it.

Joyce had said be careful. Stuart raised his head studying the onward night in all directions, lips faintly quirked. He would be careful. He had *always* been careful down here, even when he'd come with a crew of gunhandy riders, usually Arizona *vaqueros,* to take delivery of horses or cattle he'd bought over the line, but upon the occasions when he came alone, he was *very* careful. So careful in fact that he always timed his crossing to be in those dead hours before dawn when men and animals knew their lowest ebbs. He used the blending colour of his seal-brown horse, and he dressed in dark attire, as he was dressed now. He took no chances.

But this time he *had* to court peril; it was part of the reason for his coming down at all. He was confident of avoiding the customary dangers; he knew how to avoid them after all these years of doing it, but that unknown danger over the line, he was not confident about that at all. As he told the seal-brown horse when the moon was failing, ten years later he was putting his life on the line to achieve the amnesty thousands of other men had gotten in a blanket edict, and no longer even remembered, and he was trying to get it for something he had never thought was wrong and *still* did not think was wrong, which was ironic, because if he was killed this trip, he wouldn't get that pardon for doing things that, more than ten years ago, were perfectly justifiable among thousands of men who were sleeping tonight safe in their homes a thousand miles away.

Something ahead a few hundred yards

must have picked up the sound of steel shoes over gravelly soil, because without warning a small band of runty, vicious wild horses exploded out of their beds and flung away in all directions.

Stuart did not even see them, although both he and his mount detected the strong scent. There were only two kinds of wild horses, stallions and mares; each had its own gamey, wild-horse smell.

Stuart pulled up, listening to the last of those diminishing sounds, not because he cared about the wild horses, but because he wanted to know if they might have roused up any men sleeping roundabout in furtive camps. Evidently they hadn't, because long after the last echo chased itself out over the scrub-brush barrens, no fresh sound came.

He was less than two miles from the border. Except for those occasional little white cairns there was no way to be certain, unless a man was as seasoned at this ride as Jeff Stuart was.

He made the crossing like a wraith and entered Mexico without a second glance at the nearest cairn. Despite all the narrowed eyes that perpetually kept watch along here, those who knew the way knew where to make the crossing. Those who did *not* know, rarely crossed back.

Eastward, and a few miles southward, the village of Cabral stood, rude, squalid, a place of bare-bones buildings and evil-smelling back alleys. Stuart turned in that direction and kept riding, with the failing moon beginning to fade over his shoulder.

FOUR

END OF THE TRAIL

He kept the village on his left. By the time he had it in sight the night was yielding to pre-dawn's cool, aloof serenity, with no sign of life over around Cabral until the horseman headed for the stony, corpse-coloured cartroad, then a young she-goat with half a tether clinging round her neck popped out of the underbrush to stand staring. The seal-brown horse gathered up to shy, but at the last minute he caught the smell of the goat, and walked on in patent dislike, and disgust.

The goat's tawny, bulging eyes watched every move of the horse with enormous curiosity. It swallowed a sage bloom and bleated, and Jeff Stuart laughed and called back saying "Good morning to you, *chiva*."

He was a mile south of Cabral, perhaps more than a mile but there were no markers, and the road was too crooked for anyone to make a very close estimate of mileage, but he guessed it to be a mile or two, when a horseman appeared at the side of the road up ahead a hundred yards.

The man had the huge *sombrero*, lighter coloured than his dark, short *charro* jacket, and the bandoleers, of a *Rurale*. He had enormous Chihuahua rowels to his spurs, the tight, fawn-coloured trousers, and the guns, of one of those dreaded constabulary troopers. The only thing that was out of place, was his smile. *Rurales* were more dreaded than soldiers, in Mexico; they had the power of life and death without recourse to courts of law, and because they were superb horsemen, always well-mounted, they were likely to appear any-where, at any time. They were tough, deadly, cruel executioners. But as Jeff

Stuart approached this one, the man's handsome, mahogany face held its pleasant look.

He was young and lean, and rather tall for a Mexican. Also, he spoke very good English, for a Mexican. He spoke it with a faint but discernible Texas accent, and as it turned out, he possessed an excellent sense of humour, because when he said, "*Buenas dias,* pardner," and Jeff grinned, the *Rurale* raised his head and laughed at himself for blending the U.S. colloquialism with the formal Mexican greeting of "good day".

Jeff pulled up smiling. Actually, one could never be certain of *Rurales;* they quite often smiled into a man's eyes while pumping him full of lead. Only two things were undeviatingly true about them, their courage and their horsemanship. But this *Rurale,* deadly and treacherous though he might normally be, was candidly friendly now, so Jeff responded to his greeting in a similar fashion.

"Howdy, *Generál.*" And while they both smiled, he also said, "Are there lions in Guadalupe?"

The *Rurale* inclined his head gently. "*Si,* there is one; *The* lion of Guadalupe." Then he relaxed in his big-horned saddle and made a slow, appreciative study of Jeff, his horse and saddle, and lastly, most lingeringly, of his saddlebags. The last thing his dark eyes studied, was Jeff's tied-down Colt. The safety-thong was not tied in place to keep the gun from accidentally falling; this meant the gun was handy for a fast draw and the *Rurale* knew it. He raised his eyes to Jeff's face.

"Our camp is not far." He turned and led off into the thornpin-thicket without another word or glance until they were passing across a stony sand-wash and could ride stirrup, then he dropped back and asked a question.

"No trouble last night; no one trailed you?"

Jeff answered while watching a thin spindrift of soiled smoke rising pencil-thin straight up in the cool pre-dawn. "No trouble, *amigo.*"

The *Rurale* offered a mild reproof. "It was a bad thing, coming that full distance alone."

Jeff smiled. "Maybe, but the man who rides alone raises no dust."

"And you knew the way," responded the *Rurale*. "The captain told us—you are clever at border-crossing."

Jeff detected the slight antagonism in those words. "Well, *amigo,* not everyone comes down into Mexico to escape *Yanqui* law or to make trouble for Mexicans. It's true, I've made the crossing before, but never to use a gun."

The young *Rurale* shrugged that off as they came up the far side of the sand-wash.

The camp was dead ahead. There were about a dozen sleek, good animals hobbled nearby, and other Mexicans, dressed like Jeff's escort, were loafing there, eating, drinking coffee, obviously waiting. They spotted the riders instantly and turned with curiosity to study Jeff Stuart as he rode on in, stepped down, pushed back his hat, and smiled at the short, thick, pock-marked man who came to meet him. He had never met *Capitan* Herrera but Hyatt Sumner had given him an adequate description. As the officer extended a hand, Jeff shook and said, "The Lion of Guadalupe," and Herrera laughed, pleased.

"The fox of Duro," he replied, and even the *Rurales* over by the little breakfast fire, smiled. "Coffee," said Pablo Herrera, "and beans with meat. *Carne con chili.*"

Jeff stepped back, removed the saddle-bags, handed them to Pablo Herrera, then loosened the cinch of his horse, hobbled him and removed the bridle to hang it upon his saddlehorn. Finally, he went with Herrera over to the little fire and the youthful, friendly *Rurale* who had met Jeff Stuart at the side of the Cabral-road, passed over a tin plate and a dented tin cup.

Capitan Herrera went out a short way, opened the saddlebags, studied their contents, then closed them and came back to squat beside Jeff at the fire. He did not allow the saddlebags to get more than a foot from his reach, but he did not mention them, and neither did anyone else.

They talked of horses, which men like all of them were invariably did first, then they talked of other things and Jeff's Spanish was as good as theirs, which pleased them; very few *Norteamericanos* in Mexico ever bothered to learn the language of Mexico, a source of traditional antagonism among Mexicans. They also discussed politics, which, at least in Mexico, were usually impossible to untangle or to correctly assess because they changed so often and so suddenly. Finally, when they were smoking, having their second cup of coffee, *Capitan* Herrera told his men to go catch the horses and saddle up, that they would break camp soon, and when he was alone with Jeff he said, "Did the man who gave you those saddlebags tell you why they were to be brought to me?"

Jeff, fishing in a pocket for a match, felt the little badge which he had forgotten to hand over. As he answered, he dug the thing out and offered it to Herrera. "He told me what he thought I had to know. I didn't ask for more."

Herrera looked at the badge, then waved it away. "I don't need that now, *Señor.* You came. You are here. You had the saddle-bags. That little badge was only to identify you to me." Herrera's strong white teeth flashed. "Keep it as a souvenir of this conspiracy."

Jeff pocketed the badge and lit his cigarette.

Herrera looked out where his men were saddling. In a quiet, slightly menacing tone he said, "It is a lot of money in those saddlebags, *amigo*. I told Hyatt Sumner most men would count it, decide it was indeed a fortune, and would never arrive down here at all." Herrera's muddy dark eyes lingered on Jeff. "He told me he knew a man who would not only arrive down here, but who would do it without even my best men finding him until he wanted to be found."

Jeff looked around. "You had other men up along the border, *Capitan?*"

Herrera spread thick hands. "*Amigo,* what would you have done? Yes, I had them all the way up to the outskirts of Duro. It had to be that you came here."

Jeff finished his coffee, tossed the dregs into the fire, set the dented cup aside and smoked in thoughtful silence for a while. If Herrera was telling the truth, then Jeff had eluded his spies. He knew this was true because of those wild horses and those Swift-foxes; wild animals would have detected the presence of other men and simply would not have been there. He blew smoke into the chilly pale dawn. It did not matter, now, whether Herrera was trying to impress Jeff, or whether he was telling the truth; the saddlebags had been delivered, and all that remained now was for Jeff to pick up some horses on the outskirts of Cabral he had agreed to purchase from a rancher up there, and start back for Duro.

Herrera said, "You looked in the saddle-bags, *Señor?*"

Jeff had. "*Si*, I looked. Marshal Sumner told me, but I looked anyway." He smiled into the muddy dark eyes. "Be a hell of a note to be told what I was delivering, then to get down here to your camp and discover I'd been double-crossed and the saddlebags were empty."

Herrera agreed with a nod. "It would have been fatal, *amigo.*"

They laughed, then Herrera laid a hand upon the saddlebags which were beside his leg. "The men who stole that money and those jewels will be looking for it."

Jeff shrugged. "You'll be ready if they do, *Capitan.*"

Herrera's smile widened. "*Seguro.* We will be waiting. But, *amigo,* will they come down here to find it?"

Jeff tossed down his smoke. All he actually knew about the contents of the saddlebags was what Hyatt Sumner had told him when he'd first approached Jeff about making the ride down below Cabral to deliver the saddlebags. Sumner had simply said that a band of renegade Texans had raided a great rancho fifty miles below Cabral, had killed the *grande ranchero,* his wife and two of his *vaqueros,* had plundered the mansion and had fled back up over the line with almost a hundred thousand U.S. dollars-worth of diamonds, rubies, emeralds, and gold coins, and that this had almost caused an international incident between the governments of Mexico and the U.S., but that U.S. lawmen had tracked the Texans down, had killed three of them over in Texas, had recovered the plunder, and had promised to return it to the Mexicans.

Jeff told Herrera all this. The *Rurale* listened, then said, "That is what happened." He patted the saddlebags. "And now the trouble will end, I think, *amigo,* except that those outlaws were not all killed, and none of them at all were captured by your police, so, that is what I meant earlier, when I said they will come looking for their plunder.

But not down here. As you said, we will be ready and waiting. Those *Tejanos* understand that, and they know that your government is sending back the plunder. It was said in your newspapers this was to happen. It was Hyatt Sumner's idea to get rid of the plunder as quickly as he could, before the *Tejanos* could reach Duro, over in Arizona." Herrera patted the saddlebags again. "It worked very well. I think my government will thank your government." Herrera thought a moment, then shrugged thick shoulders. "Of course there is the dead *ranchero*. He had sons and loyal *vaqueros*. Even the *Rurales* cannot prevent everyone who is troubled with hatred from crossing the border. We try, but it is a very long border." Again Herrera shrugged. "But for you, *amigo,* it is over. You have done very well. You are an honest man." Herrera arose and slung the saddlebags across one shoulder. "We can ride back to the border with you," he offered. "It is a short distance."

Jeff declined. "No reason for you to have to bother, *Capitan*. I've got to pick up ten or twelve horses north of Cabral that I arranged to buy last month. I'll ride up there, get the horses, aim them towards Duro and let them run." He smiled, shook hands with the *Rurale*, then walked out to remove the hobbles from his mount, slip on the bridle, snug up the cinches, and raise a hand in a high wave as he swung up across leather, turning back in the direction of the Cabral roadway. The *Rurales* waved back.

The last he saw of them was when he reached that sand-wash he had crossed earlier, and by then, because the sun was up, finally, he was able to follow their westerly progress a short ways by the reflection of sunlight off metal.

He rode thoughtfully. Hyatt Sumner

had not told him all the story, obviously, just enough to get Jeff to agree to make the ride, and Marshal Sumner had come to Jeff Stuart because he was the best qualified man around Duro; the most trustworthy and the most likely to succeed.

Sumner had not mentioned those Texans except to say there had been one hell of a gunfight over in Texas and several of the outlaws had been killed. He had stressed the international aspects of the trouble, and it had been this, more than anything else, which had finally influenced Jeff to make the ride. If he were successful, Hyatt had said, Sumner would personally work for that amnesty Stuart desired, and because Hyatt Sumner was a respected federal lawman with friends higher up, Jeff had no doubt but that the pardon would come through.

When he reached the road leading towards Cabral, he looked back. The road was empty for miles. He also looked left and right. The land was empty in those directions as well. He settled loosely in the saddle, looped his reins, allowed the seal-brown horse to plod along under the increasing, pleasant heat, and rolled a cigarette while shrugging off all that trouble he had got involved with and which was now ended, as far as he was concerned.

No matter what those renegade Texans did, from now on that was the law's headache, not his.

FIVE

TEXANS!

J eff Stuart had visited in Cabral many times over the years and had never liked the town. It was not only that Cabral was ugly and dirty, but there was a feeling of treachery to the place, which actually was not unusual; most border towns were the same way. American outlaws stood insolently on the sidewalks, heavily armed and as dangerous as rattlesnakes, but more than that, there was the everlasting intrigue. No one trusted anyone else, and the low-caste Mexicans, the Indians and *mestizos,* lived in a constant state of fear from both the *norteamericano pistoleros,* and their own constabulary troops, the deadly *Rurales.*

Jeff rode out and around the town, encountered several young boys—*cabreros;*

goat-herders—with their browsing flocks, and with only one exception, the boys disappeared into the underbrush, fading from sight like wraiths.

That one exception, a small youngster with enormous dark eyes, stood in plain sight, staring as the *gringo* on the fine horse, rode past. Jeff waved but the small boy did not wave back.

North of Cabral the land had been browsed bare by bands of goats and sheep. There was never very much grass, even this time of year, after the late, warm rains, so cattle and horses did not do well on the open range. Grazing animals could easily starve on the desert, especially in a place like the desert around Cabral, but browsing animals, the little beasts who did not live off the ground, but who lived by eating the leaves and berries of the bushes which grow above the ground, did fairly well.

Northward, though, there were a few fenced pastures, and here, despite the shortage of water most of the year, there was some grass. Here, Jeff Stuart approached the ranch of an old Mexican named Eusebio Sanchez with whom he had been doing business for more than five years. He passed through a gate and, while still half a mile from the tree-shaded old buildings, Sanchez's half-wild, slab-sided dogs began howling, which was the old rancher's warning. By the time Jeff got close enough to see Sanchez outside, waiting, the dogs had been put on chains, which was probably a good thing because even after Jeff had swung down and had shaken the old Mexican's hand, the dogs still growled and snarled.

Eusebio Sanchez was lined and grey and sinewy with age. Old men in the cactus country never seemed to become infirm and sore with age, they seemed instead to continually dehydrate and wither until they were as fragile as dried rawhide. Sanchez was a hawk-faced old man with a grizzled mane of iron-grey hair, and a fierce horseman's moustache which he habitually tugged at when he was thinking. He took Jeff to a faggot-corral out near his adobe barn and showed him eight young horses which were obviously of better breeding than most of the horses around Cabral. But Eusebio Sanchez had not raised them, he had traded for them. He raised very few horses of his own. Around Cabral, he was a dealer in livestock exactly as Jeff Stuart was, up in the Duro country. It was through traders that they had met, and over the years they had come to respect each other. Both were shrewd horsemen and experienced traders, and so far, if either one had got the better of the other, neither had ever mentioned it, but as they leaned in tree-shade discussing the eight corraled horses, each had the look of a man intent upon making the best possible trade.

But this time Jeff had cash in his pockets. There would be no trading, actually, only bartering back and forth. It started out at the corrals; Sanchez pointed out the excellent breeding of his stock. Jeff acknowledged that the horses were indeed good stock. On the other hand he pointed out, they were only halter-broke, and green colts were not saleable until someone had invested time and money getting them trained to bit and saddle.

Eusebio Sanchez took his friend back to the *ramada*, brought out a jug of red wine, and as they sat in the serene shade, he told Jeff he would part with the eight young horses at a ridiculously low figure, simply because he realised Jeff would have to break them to saddle.

Jeff sprawled in a chair, accepted the glass of red wine, and said, "How much, then, old friend?"

In Spanish, old Sanchez said, "Because we are old friends, you can have them as though they were a gift. I am an old man much concerned for the salvation of my soul. I wish to do good deeds only."

Jeff sipped the wine, which was bitter, without changing expression. "For the salvation of your soul, then, I would offer five American dollars a head."

Old Sanchez sighed dolorously. "It is a nice figure and a generous offer," he replied, also speaking in Mexican. "Know you then, friend, that my soul is steeped in venial sin; five American dollars would not buy enough candles."

"Ten," said Jeff, still gazing woodenly off in the direction of the faggot-corral.

"Fifteen."

Jeff groaned and rolled his eyes skyward. Old Sanchez's bird-bright black eyes studied the younger man. "Twelve." he said, "and the spurs you wear."

"Ten and the spurs I wear—plus a prayer for your soul when I get back to Duro."

Sanchez looked into his glass, which was half empty. "Thirteen dollars, my son, without the spurs and without the prayer."

Jeff finally looked over. The old man suddenly laughed. They *both* laughed, and Jeff reached into a trouser pocket to count out the money. At Duro, he could hire the horses saddle-broke for ten dollars each. When he sold them, broke and bridle-wise, because they were good quality animals, he would get somewhere between thirty and fifty dollars a head for them. On the other hand, he knew old Sanchez hadn't given over five dollars, Mex, for them, so he was also doubling his money.

Sanchez re-filled their glasses and accepted the American money, then, with twinkling eyes, he said, "I am an old one with a softening brain and everyone gets the best of me."

Jeff grinned. "Yeah, I know they do. That's why you live better than anyone else around Cabral, old friend. Do you have a paper?"

Sanchez already had it written out in his pocket. All he had to do was fill in the price he had received, which he did, then handed over the bill of sale. With that done, he settled back in his chair, studied the empty, far spread of morning-lighted desert and said, "Do not take the horses straight northward. Go west twenty miles, first, then turn northward up across the border."

Jeff studied the seamed, mahogany old features in silence. Sanchez shot him a look from wise and knowing eyes.

"There were men looking for a *gringo* riding a seal-brown horse last night. They stopped here to ask. Of course I saw no such *gringo.*"

Jeff said, "*Rurales?*"

Old Sanchez shook his head. "God forbid. But no, these were *norteamericanos.*" He paused, then said, "*Tejanos.*"

Jeff felt the impact of that last word. It had not been more than three hours since he and Captain Herrera had been discussing renegade Texans. Jeff picked up his glass, sipped bitter wine for a moment in thought, then swore in English. What he did not say, but what he wondered hard about now, was how those Texans—if indeed they were *those* Texans—could have got over to Arizona so fast, and could have picked up his trail so quickly. Granting, they had that hoard of stolen wealth to motivate them, it still did not seem altogether plausible that these would be the same Texas outlaws.

It couldn't be, and yet what other Texans would be looking for a man riding south into Mexico from Duro on a seal-brown horse?

He drained the glass and declined when Eusebio Sanchez offered to re-fill it.

It *was* those Texans, and it did not matter how they had discovered Jeff Stuart had the saddlebags and was on his way southward to deliver them to Captain Herrera, what mattered was that those outlaws were somewhere between where Jeff now was, and the border. If they could catch him in Mexico, they could force him to tell what he had done with the saddlebags, then kill him, and no one in Mexico would be very greatly concerned; especially along the border where *gringos* were not well liked.

He had no doubts at all about what would happen if the outlaws caught him. They would make him talk if it took all day, a hot fire, and heated knifeblades. The fact that the Texans probably would not be able to recover their loot from the *Rurales* might not prevent them from making the effort, but that would not concern Jeff Stuart; once he told the Texans the *Rurales* had those saddlebags, they would very likely be so angered they would finish him off in a hurry.

Old Sanchez sat in silence for a long time before speaking again. "It was you they were seeking, then," he said in Spanish. "You have done something?"

Jeff gave a death's-head smile. "I have indeed done something, old friend. I have helped your government by returning plunder stolen out of Mexico by those Texans."

Sanchez held his red wine to the sun's rays and admired the blood-coloured brilliance from narrowed eyes. "Leave the horses," he eventually said. "Come back for them another time. They will be entirely safe upon my range until you come back. Wait, now, until darkness, and slip away. There is no moon and you have done this many times." Old Sanchez lowered the glass to sip from it. "You met the *Rurales?*"

"Yes. And handed over to them the plunder."

"Then why is it that they did not accompany you back?"

"They offered to, and I refused."

"Foolish," murmured old Sanchez. "Very foolish."

"Well hell," exclaimed Jeff. "I didn't know there was anyone looking for me until I rode in here and you said they were around last night."

Sanchez sighed. "This is a bad thing, my friend, that you have got involved with."

Jeff could have agreed with that. Right then, sitting in the *ramada's* pleasant springtime shade, he also decided that if Hyatt Sumner ever came to him for aid again, he would tell Sumner where to go.

But that was in the future, and right now Jeff Stuart was being skewered in the present. He arose, hitched at his gunbelt, tipped down his hat and stood a moment gazing northward and westward for signs of horsemen—dust in the golden sunlight. There was none, which was encouraging. He said, "Perhaps, old one, those gunmen—those *pistoleros*—are down in Cabral drinking cool beer and remaining in the shade."

Sanchez also arose. "If God is willing," he murmured. "You are going to take the horses?"

"Yes."

"Come then. I will help you tie them, because you will have to lead them, and slowly, otherwise they will raise dust which people can see for miles. You must lead them westward at least ten miles, before turning northward up over the line, and after that, you should turn them loose and ride hard for Duro."

That was Jeff's idea too. They went down to the corral and made rope-halters for the young horses. Only one of the colts seemed to want to fight, and Eusebio Sanchez took that one aside, dropped him hard three times with a running-w, and afterwards, with all the fight knocked out of him, the big colt stood, trembling and dripping sweat, ready to be docile.

Jeff mounted the seal-brown, gathered the lead-lines, nodded for old Sanchez to open the gate, and rode out. They did not speak to one another as they passed at the gate, but they both nodded, then Jeff turned off westerly into the desert, squinted at the sun, thought it had to be about high noon, and set his course.

He did not go northward at all. In fact, he angled a little deeper into Mexico, riding southwesterly, because he had no intention of approaching the border until after nightfall.

The heat mounted, and that helped by drying out the young horses until they were content to plod along. They were learning to be led-animals too, which would be part of their education, although under the circumstances Jeff would have just as soon not have had to bother with this at all.

He kept a narrow watch for dust back in the direction of Cabral, and saw none right up until the sun sank and it became no longer possible to discern dust. Then, with rising hope, he turned northward, heading directly for the border.

The horses were thirsty. So was their owner, but after nightfall came that would not bother any of them very much, and when he turned the young animals loose and busted them out northward, the first water-scent they would pick up would be far northward, up around Duro, so he could expect them to head in that direction. After dark he would not be able to see them, or keep up with them either. He would find them, though, tomorrow morning, on the outskirts of Duro. This was how he had been driving loose stock up out of Mexico for years. It always worked.

SIX

OUT OF THE NIGHT

He was in territory he had not ridden through in years by the time he reached the border, ten and more miles west of the Cabral road. He had seen nothing and heard nothing, and neither had the horses, so, as he approached the first pile of white-washed stones, he had no real misgivings although he scouted-up the countryside as though he had, and finally he crossed the line on an angle, heading for a thicket which lay darkly twisted and prickly a half mile or so northwesterly. He wanted to keep these thickets around him from here on.

Perhaps the Texans were still back in Cabral; he hoped they were, and most probably they were because aside from the dark-eyed girls, there were *cantinas* which served fiery Mexican liquor, and there were always gambling rooms. It would, he told himself, depend on just how fiercely motivated those Texans were, whether they would be back in Cabral relaxing, or whether they might, by now, have back-tracked him from the *Rurale* camp to the adobe of Eusebio Sanchez, and from there southwesterly.

They would not have been able to track him after sundown, and since they had not caught him by then, there was small chance that they could so in the night.

He rode through the thickets, angling northwesterly, and did not turn the young horses loose although he meant to, because by now they were content to walk along beside the seal-brown gelding as though they were old, trail-used animals.

He began to feel increasingly confident, the farther towards Duro he progressed, and the later the hour grew. No one would catch him now, unless they happened to be close enough to hear him, and even then it would not be easy, because his horses would hear, or scent, strangers in the night and give ample advance warning.

The night remained warm, and eventually a thin-bladed, curved little moon arose, but it gave very little light; he rode by starshine, but actually he had made this crossing so many times he really did not even need any light at all.

He had until dawn to cross the desert. It was a long, tedious ride, and it occurred to him that since his young horses were barefoot, they would probably be tender by the time they saw daylight again. The desert was soft, but that was deceptive because its softness was made up of billions of tiny particles of abrasives.

He made a cigarette after he had covered about ten or twelve miles, and loosened in the saddle. The night was utterly still all around him. He crossed well above that bedding-ground of the wild horses, so he did not hear nor see them. Once, where there was a great length of flat, open country, he coaxed the horses into a slow-lope, and held them to it until, upon the far end of the clearing, he again encountered thornpin underbrush. He did this four times before he got back up where the landform was familiar, and by then, with the night turning chill, and with that scimitar-moon angling away on its endless orbit, he knew exactly where he was. Surprisingly, he had made exceptionally good time. In fact, he would reach Duro before dawn, and that was something he had never done before when he'd been leading horses.

The stageroad was eastward a couple of miles, but he did not go over in that direction. It did not go all the way down to the border, but ran southward from Duro only about sixteen miles, then curved and paralleled the border, but many miles northward. It did not even approach the border until it got over in the vicinity of Nogales, for a very obvious reason; stages were the prime target of every kind of outlaw on both sides of the border. At Nogales, there was an army post, and patrols kept the stageroad under constant surveillance down that far.

Once, the young horses hung back on their leadropes, but Jeff only had a momentary bad moment because his riding horse only raised his head, then lowered it and plodded along, signifying that whatever scent had come to the horses, was nothing very serious, at least not to the seal-brown, and he knew this country, so, if *he* was not upset, there would be no reason for his rider to be upset either.

That was the only interlude that could have meant something on the entire ride.

When Jeff finally saw the dark-squat forms of Duro up ahead through the ghostly starlight, he looked back and on all sides, then wagged his head. It had come off too easily. At the best he had not anticipated anything this easy, at the worst he had anticipated a running fight, with the young horses ranging far ahead in a head-high run.

It was almost like leading a band of old broke saddle animals across someone's safe pasture. He skirted around town to the west, exactly as he had left Duro the previous night, got up to his corrals, put the young horses in, removed their rope-halters, took care of the seal-brown inside the barn, stalled him, grained and hayed him, then went back outside to pitch feed to the colts, and afterwards he shoved back his hat, leaned upon the corral and took stock of the hushed and endless night for as long as was required to smoke a cigarette.

Too easy, he told himself. Much too easy. If those outlaws had ridden hell-for-leather all the way from Texas over to Arizona, and had got the information about Jeff Stuart riding southward with the plunder into Mexico, they were not fools, and yet something along the way must have diverted them, otherwise they certainly would have made a greater effort to catch him on his ride back to Duro than they had made: that is, if they wanted him at all.

He killed the smoke and decided the outlaws were more interested in the plunder than in him, and strolled over to enter his patio where the fresh citrus-scent of his orange and lemon tree were welcome. He tossed down his hat, sank upon an old carved wooden bench, and bent to remove his spurs. That had to be it, then; the outlaws had not been after him only as long as he had their loot. Now, they were still down there in Mexico, still on the trail of the loot.

He straightened up, dropped the heavy spurs upon the bench at his side, and reached to scratch his head. Over in the scented, heavy darkness by his lemon and orange tree a lanky shadow materialised, shoved forth a blue-steel sixgun, and cocked it. Jeff did not notice the shadow, but that sound of oiled metal grating over metal made his heart freeze in mid-stroke. For two seconds he did not even breathe. The shadow was still, and it blended perfectly, but moonlight and starshine made that sixgun look wet-shiny. The man was vague but the gun was unmistakable.

Jeff did not move, he did not even lower the hand atop his head. When his breathing resumed, though, he said, very quietly, "Step out where I can see you."

The silhouette obliged, gliding clear of the citrus trees and assuming the shape of a lanky, rawboned man a few inches taller than Jeff was, and roughly the same age. The man's face, thin and angular with prominent slanting cheekbones, was hat-brim-shadowed, all but the thin, long mouth, and it showed cruelty.

Jeff let his breath out softly. He knew in his heart who that gunman was, and yet it made no sense for one of them to be up here in Duro while his friends were over the line around Cabral. "Mind if I let my hand down?" he asked, and the shadow spoke for the first time—with a slurred, border accent.

"Yeah, I mind. Put the other hand up there too."

Jeff obeyed. "What do you want?"

"First off, you just set right still," the Texan drawled, and glided round behind Jeff and lifted away his sixgun. Then the man moved off to one side and came partially around where Jeff could see him again, better this time, because he was away from the patio wall and star-light lined his lean, coppery face.

The Texan said, "Where's your saddle?"

"In the barn where I always hang it," replied Jeff.

"Saddlebags still on it?"

"No saddlebags, *amigo*." Jeff turned his head to look at the Texan. "I left them down below Cabral."

The Texan showed his teeth in a sardonic smile. "Sure you did. Only that's not what I been waiting for. Where's the stuff you took out'n them saddlebags and kept back for yourself?"

Jeff finally understood, and he had to admire their thoroughness, their shrewdness. Except that they were wrong, because he hadn't filched anything for himself. "I didn't take anything out of the saddlebags."

"You're lyin', horse trader."

"That's the gospel truth. I did not take

a single gem nor a single gold coin out of those saddlebags. I didn't even open them after I rode out of here last night."

The Texan was silent for a moment while he studied Jeff's tilted face. Then he said, "I don't believe that, mister, ain't no man livin' who'd be that stupid. You wanted a little of that for yourself."

"How," asked Jeff, "could I have got away with any of it? The law knew exactly what was in those damned saddlebags. If I'd handed them back to the Mexicans with just one gold coin missing, they'd be after me by sun up."

The Texan lowered his gun and stepped to a chair to sit down. He did not say he believed Jeff but he did not mention the saddlebags again for a while. Instead, he said, "How much did they pay you to deliver them saddlebags down to the Messicans?"

Jeff pondered. Hyatt Sumner had not

agreed to pay him anything; he was to get his amnesty, but if he told this to the outlaw, the Texan was not going to believe anything like that and Jeff knew it. He said, "Two hundred dollars."

The Texan stared. "Two hunnert . . . ? And you'd pack fifty times that much wealth down an' hand it over to the greasers for two hunnert dollars?"

Jeff wished now he'd said five hundred, but the moment he thought that, he knew the outlaw's reaction would have been the same.

"And a pardon," he exclaimed.

The Texan frowned. "Pardon?"

"I rode with General Early during the war. We burned a town up in Pennsylvania. After the war every Confederate was pardoned but those who burned that town."

The Texan listened and studied Jeff Stuart, and finally swore to himself, "Gawda'mighty, you're crazier'n a woodtick, mister. Who cares about the damned war? It come and went a lifetime ago. And you been worryin' about the Yankees lockin' you up all these years?"

Jeff did not try to defend himself. "The pardon and two hundred dollars," he said dully. He was tired; he had not slept in a long time, and he had had nothing to eat since morning at the *Rurale* camp below Cabral. Old Sanchez's wine had helped, but only for a few hours, and now that he was home again, all the tenseness, all the anxiety and fear, had drained out leaving him feeling drained dry.

The outlaw gestured with his gun. "Shed them boots, and after your pants and gunbelt. Mister, if you been lyin' about not stealin' some of that plunder, and I find it on you . . ." The gun barrel tipped up menacingly.

Jeff kicked off his boots, then had to stand to shed his trousers. For good measure he also shed his shirt and kicked them all over to the outlaw. "There's two hundred dollars in the pants pocket," he said, sitting down practically naked. "Take it, *amigo,* and get on your horse and head for the border. Maybe I'm wrong as hell, but my guess is that you are the only one of your band who's going to come out of this with even that much. The *Rurales* have those saddlebags now, and no one in his right mind would attack a squad of those bastards."

The Texan put up his gun and picked out Jeff's boots to up-end them and shake. "You don't know us fellers," he mumbled, as he searched. "No lousy *Rurales* or no one else is goin' to keep our plunder—not if we got to clean out every damned greaser barracks between here and El Paso."

The Texan made a diligent, and profane, search, came up with the two hundred dollars, which he pocketed, then kicked the clothing back and said, "Put it on, cowboy, then you'n me are going south."

Jeff stared. "South!"

"Yeah; down to Cabral, and you're going to point out the Messicans you give them saddlebags to."

Jeff sat staring until the Texan drew his sixgun, then Jeff began to dress himself again.

SEVEN

THE RAWBONED BAY

Jeff tugged his breeches and boots back on thoughtfully. There was something about this affair which was beginning to fit a familiar patter, and regardless of his earlier thoughts about those Texans possibly being diverted, obviously, they had *not* been diverted, they had *not* chosen to follow him back northward out of Mexico, so he had been in no danger at all, last night, but they *had* demonstrated a lot more canniness than he had attributed to them. Something about all this was familiar.

They had assumed Jeff Stuart was an average border-dweller, which was a perfectly reasonable assumption. But above all else, they had *not* acted as Jeff Stuart had felt they would probably act; they hadn't bothered to try and track him down, they had out-thought him. Had had a member of the band waiting at Jeff's residence up in Duro.

They had not made a chase, nor put anyone under strain. They had not even sweated-up a damned horse, they had purely and simply out-manoeuvered Jeff Stuart by having one of their band loafing on Jeff's patio, waiting.

As he finished dressing he rolled a cigarette, offered the makings to the Texan, who declined, then asked if he could get something to eat from the kitchen. The Texan agreed, but not with much good grace, and only after Jeff had stressed the fact that he hadn't had a decent meal since the previous day.

Inside, the Texan stayed behind Jeff most of the time, and ordered Jeff not to light one of the coal-oil lamps, but to light a candle instead. Candle-light was too weak to carry far.

Jeff boiled some coffee, fried some meat and spuds, and set a bottle of Mexican chocolate brandy upon the table. Throughout all this the Texan leaned upon a wall, watching, but when Jeff finally sat down the Texan got a cup, filled it with coffee, then brought that, and a crockery plate to the table with him, and also ate. He did not touch the chocolate brandy and when Jeff held up the bottle, the Texan sneered.

"Men don't drink that stuff, only old ladies. Men drink whisky—or *tequila.*"

Jeff went back to eating and did not say a word for a while, not until he was nearly finished, not until the discomfort of being hungry had departed, then he rolled another smoke, sipped coffee, studied the outlaw and said, "Your boss say to fetch me back down to Cabral?"

The Texan nodded without speaking.

For a man who had refused to eat earlier, he was doing very well now.

Jeff finished his coffee. "You got any idea what it's going to be like, crossing that southward desert now, during broad daylight?"

The Texan raised pale grey eyes. "Mister, I've crossed as many gawd-damned deserts as you have. If you're figurin' to scare me, forget it."

"I wasn't thinking of the heat nor the lack of water," replied Stuart. "I was thinking that by now, down around Cabral, they know a band of *gringos* have crossed over. They got Mex route-armies and *Rurales* down there, not to mention *gringo* bounty-hunters and Mex *pistoleros*. Maybe your friends can make it, if they stick together, but the chances of you and me, just two men, even getting across the line—in broad daylight—are lousy."

The Texan finished eating and reached,

left-handed, for his coffee. He did not raise his right hand from under the table. He hadn't shown that right hand since sitting down opposite Jeff. Nor did he reply to Jeff, now, either. He finished off the coffee and reared back to arise.

Jeff tried once more. "Mister, it won't be worth it."

The Texan stood up. "What won't?"

"Trying to take me back down there. I already told you, I gave those saddlebags to the *Rurales*. By now your friends know that. They've probably identified which band of *Rurales* have the saddlebags. What the hell good will I be, down there?"

The Texan smiled. "More good down there, cowboy, than you'll be up here, scaring up a posse and sendin' word to the army we're in the country, and what we're after. And there's somethin' else; I got to meet 'em down there. We sure as hell ain't comin' back up through here again, when we head out after getting back our loot. You'll be my protection. Anyone gets in my way, horsetrader, they're goin' to have to shoot through you to get at me. Now cut out the damned palaverin' and let's get saddled up." The Texan did not draw his sixgun, but he laid a hand lightly upon it. "Get up and lead the way to the corrals. My saddle'n bridle are hid under some feed sacks in the barn. I'll ride that big seal-brown you come in on. You can pick out some other critter. Let's go."

Jeff arose. "Not the seal-brown. He's been down and back. That's a hundred miles practically non-stop. He'll give out on you half way to the border if you try pushing him today."

The Texan was indifferent about what he rode. "All right. Walk ahead of me an' when we get down there, point out the next best animal you got."

They left the house with the sky turning

a shade of washed-out dirty blue off in the east. Around them, the town had not come to life yet, although a dog barked somewhere southward, on the west side of the roadway, probably signifying that someone had come out of a house to feed a horse or milk a cow; if the dog was over in Mextown, maybe that householder had come forth in sandals to feed some goats.

The sun would be another half to three-quarters of an hour arising, but daylight, wan and weak and watery though it appeared, was spreading gradually over the outward desert. Jeff paused outside his adobe barn to scan the drowsing town which lay mostly southward, and to his left, the endless sweep and flow of thorny desert. For some totally unconnected reason he also thought of John Stedman's niece, but she seemed so totally unrelated, so completely alien to everything with which he had become associated over the past twenty-four hours, he only dwelt upon her for a moment, then walked on inside the barn.

The Texan went at once to uncover his saddle. It was one of those A-fork rigs with the rigging on the outside, up both sides of the fork and aft, across the sills of the saddletree behind the cantle. It was a typical Texas A-fork outfit. Only the bridle with its silver-overlayed bit, showed the Mexican, Southwestern, influence. That, and the doubled Navajo blanket. As the outlaw pulled his rig from beneath the sacking, "What horse?"

Jeff jerked his head sideways, indicating the colts in the corral outside. "Take your pick. I'll ride that rawboned bay." As Jeff spoke he collected his outfit and walked back outside. The Texan was right behind him. The young horses were awake, having been aroused by the appearance of men, but they did not act as though the big feed they'd had and the short rest had made much difference; they still seemed drawn out.

The Texan waited until Jeff had opened the gate, then he lugged his outfit on through, dropped it in the dust and stood, hands on hips, studying the horses. Finally he said, "*I'll* ride that big bay. You take something else."

Jeff offered no argument. The rawboned big bay colt had been the one, back in Sanchez's corral, which had wanted to fight, and which had been cowed only after Sanchez had dumped him head-first a few times with a running-w.

If any horse among those green colts would fight, it would be that one.

Jeff took his bridle and went forward, past the Texan, as he said, "These horses have only been topped off a few times, so take it easy with them. But they're tough as hell. They're also the only horses I've got on the place right now, except my old, worn-out seal-brown."

The Texan snorted. "I'll take it easy with that sonofabitch." He scooped up his bridle and walked ahead. Jeff expected trouble, but if there was one unpredictable thing about unbroke horses, it was their unpredictability; the same colt that would fight like a tiger one morning, would be docile as a lamb the next. A man never really knew, until he slammed a hard saddle across a cold back, what he had a handful of.

Jeff selected a fine-boned sorrel. Of all the Sanchez horses, he had, on the long, tedious ride up from Mexico, decided he liked the rawboned bay, a short-back, burly little pigeon-toed brown, and the fine-boned sorrel, best. He anticipated little trouble with the sorrel, although he had very little doubt that somewhere between Duro and the border, either he or the

Texan, and perhaps both of them, would have a horseback-adventure. He did not doubt that the colts could make that trip back down there, even though by now they had to be tenderfooted, because they were young and strong and resilient, but neither did he really believe he and the Texan would make it over the line without something happening.

As he eased up to catch the fine-boned sorrel, he watched the Texan from the corner of his eye. Obviously, the outlaw was a horseman; maybe not a polished nor finished one, but at least a lifelong one, because as soon as he had the rawboned bay backed into the faggots at the far end of the corral, he talked his way up and never moved fast, not even when he eased up a hand to loop leather around the animal's neck, close to the gullet.

Bitting a colt that had never had cold steel in its mouth before usually did not occur until long after the horse had been broke to saddle and taught to rein through the use of a hackamore, or, as the Mexicans called it, a *jaquima*. It was a gentle gradual process. This morning there were no hackamores, and no time. The Texan thumbed open his mount's mouth, slid in the bit being careful not to strike teeth, and Jeff was surprised, both at the man's expertise, and at the fact that the rawboned bay, although it rolled its eyes and stood wide-legged, did absolutely nothing. Even when the Texan led the bay over where his saddle and blanket lay, near the gate, the bay still did nothing.

Perversely, the moment Jeff tried to bit the fine-boned sorrel, the animal struck at him. He fought it back to a corner, always keeping slightly to one side of the striking fore-feet, and even when the sorrel reared and tried to lunge past, Jeff persevered. The Texan laughed and Jeff swore. *This* was the horse he would have wagered money would not fight a man.

He got the sorrel bitted. The shock of cold steel in its mouth made the sorrel freeze in his tracks. He would not move. Jeff had to go over, pick up his saddle, and go back. Still the sorrel did not move. He stood like stone even while the saddling process was under way, his only movement rolling eyes and slightly distended nostrils.

The Texan turned his bay horse several times. It was entirely tractable. The Texan led his animal over and stood, hands on hips, as Jeff tried to move his sorrel off centre. The horse would not budge. He was braced and rock-set in his tracks.

There was a way to untrack him. Jeff stepped to the sorrel's shoulder, sucked back, then jolted the horse hard by hurling his body, shoulder up, against his front end. The sorrel yielded, but only a yard, then he took another stubborn stance.

The Texan looked down. "Where are your spurs?"

"On the patio, where I left them," said Jeff, annoyed at the horse almost as much as he was at the Texan. He checked the sorrel, swung up, eased down across the sorrel's back—and for some totally inexplicable reason the sorrel loosened all over. Jeff waited for the explosion. It did not come. When he squaw-reined to the right, the sorrel ewe-necked around, but he also obediently responded to the pressure and turned. Jeff squeezed with his knees and squaw-reined to the left, towards the gate. The sorrel turned and walked in that direction. Jeff looked back. "Well," he said, "are you going to stand there, or are we going south? That damned sun's going to be hot; the more ground we cover before it gets high, the better."

The Texan turned, cheeked his bay, lunged up over leather and dropped hard down in the saddle. It was a needlessly rough mount. It triggered something deep within the rawboned bay's little brain—and he fired.

For one short moment, as the Texan warily eyed those small ears, there was nothing. Then the bay locked his jaws and plunged downward with his head before the Texan could even-up his reins and take a short hold to prevent the horse from having his head. In that same moment the bay bawled like an enraged stallion, sprang his legs a little and shot straight into the air. When he came down, with the Texan sawing hard in an effort to hurt the bay's mouth so that he would lift his head, the bay sunfished hard left. The Texan desperately jammed his left leg straight to retain balance. The bay spun right. The Texan, no longer fighting the reins, simply trying to stay aboard, jammed down hard with a stiff right leg—and the bay hurled himself almost straight upwards on his hind legs.

Jeff held his breath. Usually, young horses, which did not have stiff ankles or tendons, did not go over backwards, and probably this one would not have, except that the Texan, unable to grab the horn, used the reins to try and stay in the saddle, and pulled the colt over.

Jeff was on the ground almost before the bay hit, smashing the Texan's saddle when his full weight came down upon it, backwards. Many men had been killed this way; saddlehorns with a thousand pounds behind them, had been driven through many a breastbone.

What saved the Texan's life was that he was still sagging to his right from the bay's previous manoeuvre; when he fell, he fell sideways, both feet clear of the stirrups. The horse rolled left, the man rolled right, and the Texan's gun and hat skidded through the dust as Jeff ran close.

The horse scrambled back to his feet and pitched violently away. The Texan lay there, mouth wide, eyes dark with shock, half the breath knocked out of him.

Jeff picked up the Colt, cocked it, and waited.

EIGHT

A CHILLING REVELATION

Hyatt Sumner was draping his hat across the wall-peg beside the gun-rack in his office next door to the Duro jailhouse when someone kicked open the door and stamped in.

He turned and stared, first at the dishevelled, lanky man hatless and gun-less, who came first, then at Jeff Stuart who had stiff-armed the hatless man ahead and entered last, kicking the door closed behind them. Jeff's right hand with the cocked Colt in it, wig-wagged for the pale, lanky man to cross the room and sit upon the wall-bench.

Marshal Sumner turned, went to his desk and stood there. Gazing at the Texan he said, "Who the hell is he?"

Jeff, eyeing his prisoner, said, "I don't

know his name, but I can tell you one thing he *isn't*—a bucking-horse rider."

The Texan's pale grey eyes showed murder in their depths as he gazed steadily and soundlessly at his captor.

Jeff explained how the Texan had been waiting for him when he returned from the border; he also told Marshal Sumner about the outlaw band of which this Texan was a member, and he concluded with his report of having delivered the saddlebags to Pablo Herrera at the camp below Cabral.

Then he said, "You didn't mention these damned outlaws heading this way, Marshal. All you told me was that our government wanted that plunder returned to the Mexicans. You came within an ace of getting me killed."

Hyatt Sumner stepped round to the chair behind his desk, using this short moment as the means for collecting his thoughts. After sitting down he spread both hands upon the desktop and gazed from his dark eyes at Jeff.

"The plain truth, Jeff, is that although I received word some of them got clear after the gunfight over in Texas, all anyone thought was that they *might* try and get the plunder back. I didn't *know*, for a fact, that they were coming. And that's the gospel, so help me."

Jeff kept scepticism to himself. He and Hyatt Sumner could wrangle over this some other time. "You didn't know they rode into Duro, and someone who knew I'd ridden out night before last, told them?"

Instead of answering, Marshal Sumner turned towards the Texan. Only the second part of Jeff's statement evidently interested him. "Who did you talk to here in Duro?" he asked.

The Texan sat back giving look for look, and saying nothing. Jeff had not thought he was a fearful man; now, in the hands of the law, he did not show any trepidation at all.

Sumner continued to study the man. "You'll tell me, cowboy, sooner or later."

The Texan said, "Tell you nothing," and sneered.

Hyatt Sumner's dark eyes unblinkingly regarded the Texan through a quiet moment, then the deputy U.S. marshal arose and said, "I don't think I'll lock you up," and at the baffled look he got from the Texan about that, Sumner smiled thinly. "The Mexicans'll be getting out their own posters on your band within a day or two. I think I'll just chain you up and deliver you down to the border."

The Texan's expression subtly changed. The deep and enduring, and mostly silent, hatred Mexicans had for Texans went back a long time—to the bloody and triumphant insurrection of the Texans against Mexico, and to the subsequent scorn and contempt with which Texans had afterwards continually showed towards Mexicans. In Mexico, where anti-Americanism was not really endemic nor virulent, except at unpredictable and frenzied intervals, at least far inland, up along the border where there *was* an enduring antipathy, it was focused mostly upon Texans.

And there was one other thing; Mexicans were naturally callous and cruel. They still practised torture, never openly, never as a national policy, but they practised it and everyone knew they practised it. Hyatt Sumner continued to thinly and malevolently smile.

"I'll ask you once more, and if you don't want to answer it'll be all right with me, *Tejano.* I'll deliver you to the *Rurales* by tomorrow morning. Who told your headman Stuart rode out of Duro night before last?"

The Texan countered with a question of

his own. "And if I tell you?"

Sumner eased back down in his chair. "The Mexicans won't get you. That's all."

The outlaw looked at Jeff, briefly, then swung back towards Hyatt Sumner. "A greaser over in Mex-town who was sneakin' back home after dark, and walked right up into our camp where we was waitin' for nightfall, a couple of miles out. He'd stoled some goats and had taken them to a dry-wash out five or six miles. He seen a feller ridin' out on a seal-brown horse, had watched him head southward out a ways from town, and had watched because he knew the feller—it was Stuart. The Messican seen the saddlebags." The Texan paused. "And he seen something else—you and Stuart sneakin' around in an alleyway for a rendezvous earlier."

Jeff scowled faintly. "From that your leader figured out I was delivering the plunder?"

The Texan's wide, bloodless wound of a mouth pulled wider in a mirthless, knowing smile. "Horsetrader, the feller who's doing the thinkin' for us, don't need no more. We been following the trail of them saddlebags a damned long while. We knew when they come to Duro. Maybe you're lucky, Marshal; if you'd still had that plunder, by yesterday morning they'd have found you around here somewhere with your throat cut."

"Why here?" asked Jeff. "Why in Duro?"

"Because, damn it all, there's been army patrols or stages full of marshals," stated the Texan. "We wasn't sure there wouldn't be a company of cavalrymen here in Duro, neither. That's why we stayed out of town and sent a couple of men in to scout up the place, first. Hell, if we'd known they'd just hand the plunder over to one man, here in Duro, believe me, we'd have hit this damned village like a whirlwind. Then that goat-thief got caught wanderin' around out there near our camp, and we figured out the rest of it. Stuart; you was just plain lucky. You too, Marshal."

Hyatt Sumner looked at Jeff. "The Mex can wait. We'll get to him later. Right now I'm going to lock this one up, then send word over to Nogales about the others. If they get lucky down in Mexico and get that damned loot back, they'll probably head northeast over in the direction of El Paso. If they get back up into Texas . . ." Hyatt Sumner left his sentence unfinished, purposefully; there was a prevailing conviction elsewhere in the West, as well as the North and East, that Texans protected Texans. It had been proven true innumerable times. Texas was an insular, hidebound place, full of strong prejudices and enduring animosities towards outsiders, particularly against Mexicans, outside lawmen, and the Union.

Maybe, as the prisoner had told Jeff last night, the war had been a lifetime ago, but deep down, very few Texans really felt that way; they had the grudge, and they had no intention of relinquishing it. Not yet, anyway.

The prisoner smiled at Marshal Sumner. "You ain't going to do nothin'. Nogales is quite a spell from here. By the time they get a message down there, from you, it'll be all over."

Jeff thought that was probably right, but not the same way the Texan thought it would be over. Jeff remembered Pablo Herrera and those other heavily armed, cruel-faced *Rurales*. He said nothing, though; he simply holstered the Texan's sixgun and strolled to a window to gaze out into the roadway. He was no longer hungry, but he was still dog-tired. This feeling had returned, once he had sat down in the marshal's office, the last vestiges of that earlier excitement at the corral dying out, leaving the earlier weariness stronger than ever.

John Stedman came out of the general store, across the way, looked at the sun, looked at his pocket-watch, then surveyed the cool, morning-lighted roadway and turned to stroll back into the store. There was no sign of Joyce Kincaid.

Sumner said, "What's your name?" to the prisoner, and got back an indifferently drawled response.

"Jesse James."

Sumner coloured slightly, then tried again. "What's your name, *Tejano?*"

This time the prisoner stared insolently before replying. "You fixin' to beat it out of me, Marshal?"

Jeff turned. He knew Hyatt Sumner. The Marshal arose, deliberately unbuckled his gunbelt, lay it atop the desk, removed his coat and started around the desk. Jeff said, "Texas, you better answer. I've seen him half-kill a lot bigger and tougher men than you are."

The Texan pulled up straight over where he sat, as though to arise, then he suddenly said, "Will Ray Scarbrough," and Jeff forgot all about Hyatt Sumner to stare.

"Do you have a brother?" asked Jeff.

The outlaw, still warily watching Marshal Sumner, who had stopped in mid-stride beyond the corner of his desk, flashed a sidewards look at Jeff. "Yeah, I got me a brother."

Jeff stepped back to the chair he had vacated and sat down again. "Is your brother's name Morgan Scarbrough?"

The outlaw, satisfied now that Sumner was not coming, rocked back and put a pale grey stare across the room towards Jeff Stuart. "Yeah. Morg's my brother. You know him?"

Jeff turned. "Hyatt . . . ?"

Marshal Sumner was shrugging back into his coat, his face still red and rock-set. "I got ten flyers on Morgan Scarbrough," stated Sumner, picking his gunbelt off the desktop and flinging it around his middle again.

But that wasn't what had surprised Jeff. He knew, as well as most other people west of the Missouri knew, that Morgan Scarbrough led a band of very deadly and very successful outlaws; that he was notorious all across the Southwest. What Jeff Stuart remembered, and what now made him lean back studying the prisoner, remembering that last night he had thought there had been something vaguely familiar about all this, was that Morgan Scarbrough had been a guerilla commander of Confederates back during the war. Last night, what had seemed illusively familiar, and what had fallen into place so perfectly now that Morgan Scarbrough's name had cropped up, was that the band of outlaws who were trying to retrieve their plunder, were functioning exactly like irregular soldiers, even to planning ahead by leaving one of their group in Stuart's patio.

He told himself that the whole damned thing had been planned, not by kill-crazy renegades, but by one of the most successful and daring guerilla leaders of the Lost Cause. He kept staring at the Texan. "Morgan Scarbrough. *Colonel* Morgan Scarbrough. What did you tell me last night; the war was a lifetime ago and no one remembered it any more?"

Sumner was rummaging in a box of wanted posters and ignored this exchange when the prisoner said, "No one *does* remember it, Stuart. We're livin' in a different time."

Jeff slowly shook his head at the Texan. "Yeah; a different time—but the same rules apply." Then Jeff turned. "Hyatt . . . ?"

"Yeah? I can't find those damned flyers on the Scarbrough bunch."

"Listen, damn it," exclaimed Jeff. "Morgan Scarbrough isn't going to high-tail it for Texas, whether he gets that damned plunder back or not."

Sumner looked up. "Why not?"

Jeff pointed. "That's his damned brother you've got in custody. That's why not!"

NINE

MOONLIGHT AND
A SORREL HORSE

Marshal Sumner took Will Ray Scarbrough next door and locked him into a jailhouse cell, and although the captured outlaw was garrulous, now that he had finally begun to talk, Marshal Sumner's reaction to having the brother of perhaps the most notorious outlaw-leader in the Southwest on his hands, was exactly the opposite. He would not even respond to the enquiry of a man he met on his way out of the jailhouse who was the part-time Town Marshal of Duro, who had every right to know who had been locked up in there.

Jeff Stuart returned to his home at the upper end of town, got the saddles off the two horses he had left with the other loose-stock in the corral, and went inside to sleep.

He did not awaken until evening, and he might not have awakened then, except that someone came to bang upon his roadside door. It was Henry Steele, the gunsmith, who also filled in, occasionally, as local lawman. But this evening he came in a different capacity. Standing in Jeff Stuart's doorway the old gunsmith said, "Jeff, there's a rumour round town that the feller you handed over to Hyatt Sumner is the brother of Morgan Scarbrough. Well; folks are wonderin'—is he or ain't he?"

Jeff thought he knew why the gunsmith was there, but instead of alluding to that, he simply nodded his head. "He is Morgan Scarbrough's brother, Henry."

Steele did not alter expression, but he had his next remark poised for delivery. "Well then, damn it, we got to get him out of Duro. Someone's got to take him on the stage down to Nogales, and the word's got to be spread round that he ain't here, that he's down there."

Jeff understood, perfectly, but he acted as though he didn't. "Why?"

"Because, confound it, Morgan Scarbrough ain't just one of your penny-ante *buscaderos,* Jeff, and you know he ain't. If he knew we had his brother in our jailhouse . . . Last time I seen him mentioned in a newspaper it had to do with a big fight out in the roadway, somewhere down in Texas, his crew against a flock of lawmen. Jeff, Morgan Scarbrough's got maybe as many as ten outlaws riding with him. A place like Duro ain't no army post. We can't be expected to stand up to—"

"Wait a minute, Henry; why tell me all this? Hyatt Sumner's got Scarbrough in custody, I haven't."

Old Steele looked testily at the younger man. "I know that, confound it. I'm here because the citizens of Duro are organisin' to go in a body to Hyatt and make him get that damned outlaw out of this town. We want you to march down there with us."

Jeff considered the gunsmith through a long interval of silence, then said, "If you've got everyone else, Henry you sure as hell don't need me."

Steele's grizzled brows dropped a degree. "You're for keeping that bastard here in town?"

"Not necessarily, Henry, but I just got a bad feeling, when you said someone was going to have to ride the stage down to Nogales with Scarbrough. I've already done my civic duty for this month."

Steele's brows lifted slightly. "Naw, we wouldn't ask you to do that. In fact, John Stedman's been selected by our citizens vigilance committee."

Jeff stared. "John? Does he know this?"

"No. But we're going to tell him as

soon—"

"Henry, what the hell are you trying to do? John Stedman's the *last* man around Duro to ride shotgun on a man like Will Ray Scarbrough."

Steele shrugged. "Well, can't be helped. Hyatt won't do it."

"Have you asked him?"

"No. But I know he won't do it anyway. He's never yet ridden gun-guard on a prisoner that's been sent down to the army at Nogales. He's forever sayin' this here is his post, and let someone else do the shot-gun riding after he catches 'em." The gunsmith leaned upon the doorjamb. "Anyway, we don't have to sweat about that just yet; first things first. We'll be rallyin' in an hour or such a matter at Murphy's saloon. You be there, Jeff; we need you. In fact we need everyone we can get." Steele raised a gnarled finger. "We got to get that bastard out of Duro before his brother finds out we

got him and comes down here a-shootin'
and a-hollerin'."

The gunsmith turned and hiked back
towards the centre of town.

Jeff stood a moment longer in the
doorway, then turned away, closed the
door, swore, and went to the washhouse
out back where he could scrub off desert-
dust and travel-stain while he did some
thinking. It was later, when he was shaving,
that he felt the most disgust with Henry
Steele and whomever Henry was working
up this vigilance committee with. Why
hadn't they gone, first, to Hyatt Sumner?
Hyatt could have told them where Morgan
Scarbrough was, and what Scarbrough's
chances were of getting back up out of
there alive.

He left the house after feeding his
horses, and went down through a bland
night with a slightly thicker moon, to have
supper at a café. Afterwards, he went up

towards Murphy's *Sahuaro Saloon*, not to join the vigilantes but to watch from the shadows across the road and see how many showed up, and as he built a smoke and ducked his head to light up, a slim, lithe shadow loomed in front of him. He raised his eyes.

The taffy hair and the gold-tanned face were like a brush-stroke painting of a lovely woman's soft-smiling face against a sooty background of early nightfall. He dropped the match and straightened his stance.

"You said three or four days," she told him. "I saw you come out of the marshal's office this morning."

He regarded her soberly, not because his mood was grave but because, being this close to her again was like being close to a cool breeze on a blasting hot day, or like seeing blue water in the mid-August desert; it was something to feel, to admire, to wonder about, more than it was something to smile at.

"Made it down and back in record time," he said.

"You brought back some horses?"

He nodded. "Eight head," then, on a sudden inspiration, remembering that she had rebuffed his offer to fetch back something for her, he said, "There's one in particular I'd like to show you?"

She gazed a little warily at him. "Where are they?"

"In the corrals out back of my place." He held out a hand. This was the way they had walked together that first night they had met. It seemed appropriate now. She looked down, then up, looked as though she would laugh, and took his hand in her cool fingers.

They had to cross the road, but he made no attempt to do that until they were well northward, up nearer his residence, where the town was quieter and there were fewer people abroad. He forgot all about the meeting down at the saloon. He took her around past the low wooden gate leading to his patio, across in front of the adobe barn to the faggot-corral, and there, finally, he released her hand and pointed to the fine-boned sorrel gelding. "That one," he said.

She leaned at his side, the clean, soap-scent of her hair almost painfully clear to him, and stared at all the horses, then looked longest at the sorrel. "He's afraid," she said softly.

The sorrel horse had reason to be fearful, but Jeff said nothing of this. "He'll be all right. What he needs is a friend."

"Can you ride him?" she asked, turning slightly.

Jeff stared at the sorrel. *He* had ridden him, today, but only across the corral, and only because the horse had been too con-fused to do otherwise than let a man straddle him. Let that sorrel horse stand a day and a night thinking about being ridden, and the next time someone tried it, the rider might get one hell of a surprise. Jeff turned, grinning a little ruefully. "Well—in time he could be ridden, but he's not a broke horse yet." He kept looking at her. The way that slightly thicker moon was casting down light across her lifted, golden-tanned face, made her look even younger than she was; younger and more lovely.

"He's yours, Joyce."

She blinked, then seemed almost as confused as the sorrel had seemed, earlier. She looked down, then she stole a glance across where the fine-boned breedy animal was standing, warily watching the two-legged creatures, then she eased slightly along the corral to put a little more differ-ence between them, and finally she said, "I couldn't accept him, Jeff. I really couldn't."

He studied her profile, the graceful rise of her neck and the rounded fullness of her jaw and mouth. He thought of taking her to the patio gate—but not yet. "Can't you?" he said. "Mind telling me why not?"

"Well; we don't even know each other, do we?"

He pretended to be confused. "What's that got to do with it? Look; there are eight horses in the corral. I've got another one in the barn. They're going to eat me out of house and home before I can peddle them. And besides, I got this one practically free; I only paid what about four or five of them are worth. Joyce—I just plain don't want him." He saw her eyes swivel round to his face, not really believing him, so he tried even harder. "Do you know how the cowmen up north in the grass country kill off predatory coyotes and wolves and such-like?"

"No."

He pointed to the sorrel horse. "They take a horse, lead it out a few miles, shoot it, cut it open and shove arsenic inside its stomach." He looked around slowly at her.

She was staring at him, horrified.

He said, "Will you take him?"

She still stared. "You wouldn't. Jeff Stuart you couldn't possibly do that to a horse."

"I didn't say I did it. *I* said the cowmen—"

"You wouldn't sell that beautiful animal to anyone who would do that to it. I don't believe you for one minute!"

He pushed back his hat. "Will you take it, Joyce?"

"No!"

"Yes you will."

". . . Yes I will."

He laughed and reached for her hand, but she stepped farther away, her gunmetal eyes opened wide. "Have you sold horses to the cowmen to be used—like that, Jeff?"

He hadn't. At least, he had never *know-ingly* done it. How did a man who had been around livestock all his life—explain to a beautiful girl who only knew the superficial realities of life, that there came a time in the life of every horse, of every *animal*, when death was preferable to life? A man didn't, so he said, "I have never owned a horse I couldn't find something about him that I didn't approve of. I can't say as much for the people I've known. No, Joyce, I wouldn't sell a horse who was young and healthy to anyone at all, if I figured they'd abuse him." He winked at her. "Maybe that's why I'll never be rich." He leaned, looking back into the corral. "But I've sure had a lot of horses who were friends of mine. That's better'n money anyway."

She moved back closer again, but not too close, and also leaned to look over the top of the corral. For a while neither of them spoke, but eventually she said, "But—what can I *do* with him? I've never even touched an unbroke horse. I wouldn't know where to begin . . . And I think I'd be afraid to try."

Jeff, remembering how fast the sorrel could strike, nodded his head approvingly. "As long as you continue to be a little afraid of him, you'll get along right well with him." He turned. "Tell you what I'll do; for a fee I'll help you break him to saddle."

She straightened back off the corral. "What fee?"

"One smile a day."

She looked, then she laughed, and when he held out his hand she took it again. He would have taken her over to the patio then, but she dug in her heels and held back. "I've got to get home. I told my uncle I was going for a walk. He'll be expecting me. I don't want to worry him."

Jeff said, "Just do one thing for me; go stand in that archway over there where the wooden half-door is."

She looked around. "There?"

"Yes."

She was quizzical. "Just—stand there?"

"Yes. I'll wait here."

She walked over, pushed the low door back, turned back facing him in the starshine and moonlight, and did not move.

She was perfect; no other woman he could imagine, would ever belong so perfectly. He said, "All right. Now I'll walk you home."

She let him hold her hand as they strolled back out front, and once she looked at him with a slightly baffled expression, but she did not say anything.

TEN

LAST ENCOUNTER OF THE DAY

Stuart did not linger after he walked Joyce Kincaid home, primarily because he felt like relaxing in the solitude of his patio, and partly because, since he had never cared much for noisy throngs, he decided to bypass Murphy's saloon tonight. Evidently Henry Steele's hoped-for throng had showed up, over there.

After he got home, though, he did not go at once to the house. It was too fine a night and he did not feel the slightest bit sleepy, so he walked out to the corral and leaned there, gazing over at the Sanchez-horses.

He also thought of something else. Perhaps it didn't make a whole lot of sense, and probably every man had some different idea about the kind of woman he wanted—someday—but after Jeff Stuart had acquired the *alcalde* adobe, he had, somewhere along the line between then and later, evolved a vague silhouette in his mind about the kind of woman who would fit his house and his lifestyle.

It really wasn't anything he'd sat evenings thinking about. It was, instead, something part intuitive, part fantasy, part instinctive desire. She hadn't ever really come down from the shadows of his reveries so that he could see her face, but she *had* evolved sufficiently so that he knew that when he saw her, preferably standing on his patio, or just standing in the opening of the patio gateway, he would know her. *Then,* he would be able to identify her face.

Tonight, it had happened.

He stood in the moonlight at the corral with the long silence of the outward desert reaching this far, and imagined how it

would be, him, her, and the fine-boned
sorrel horse. He smiled a little, plotting
ahead; any man who had saddle-broke
enough horses had evolved some kind of
pattern for inducing other animals to
follow his lead. A man who had out-
thought enough horses had devised a
system for imposing his will without really
seeming to. Once this became habit, it was
a natural reaction, and, uniquely enough,
although its basic purpose was to influence
four-legged critters, something any horse-
breaker knew it also worked with *two*-
legged critters.

He turned, rolled a smoke, hooked one
boot-heel over the lower stringer of the
faggot-corral, lit up, and blew smoke at the
farthest star. He had all night to indulge
himself in reveries, if he chose to do that. It
was a pleasant feeling, and it was accompanied by pleasant thoughts, until, about an
hour after he'd returned home, someone

came walking along out front, and since he was spur-less, whoever he was, obviously, he was not a rangerider nor a horsehunter, the two most common types on the south desert in the springtime. Only the horse-hunters, the mustangers, also called wild-horse trappers, remained on the south desert after springtime passed. Cattle drifted back to the northward grasslands when the desert dried up. The rangeriders, then, had no reason to come down into the desert.

This man did not stop out front, which signified that he was no stranger. When he ambled round the north side of the house into the back-lot, and Jeff got a good long look at his moving shape, he sighed, dropped the cigarette and ground it under-foot. Hyatt Sumner. He let the marshal get mid-way between barn and patio then spoke so that Sumner would see him in the corral-gloom.

"Past your bedtime, Marshal."

Sumner looked, looked harder, placed Jeff from his voice and came across the yard past the adobe barn. "Picked up some news from the northbound stage I figured you might be interested in. Scarbrough rode into a trap below Cabral."

Jeff was not completely surprised, for although Morgan Scarbrough had proven himself a wily guerilla for many years, there was something down in Mexico he might possibly have anticipated, but against which he really could produce no good defence, and that, simply stated, was Mexican antipathy. Even the pepper-bellies who did not like *Rurales,* which had to be just about every other Mexican, disliked Texans, *gringo pistoleros* of any kind, even more. If Sanchez had known there was a band of *Yanqui* riders down around Cabral, then others had also known, and someone would have carried the word to Pablo Herrera, whose natural reaction would not be to ride out and face the *Tejanos,* not even courageous *Rurales* were likely to do that, very often. Captain Herrera's reaction would be a very professional ambuscade, which was something else the *Rurales* were very good at working out.

When Jeff stood in thought, Marshal Sumner gave more details. "Scarbrough had eight men with him. The Mexicans baited him by sending in some pepperbelly with a hint that he knew where the band of *Rurales* were in camp who had your saddlebags." Sumner paused, looking steadily over, then he wagged his head. "I wouldn't have believed Morgan Scarbrough could have been taken down the path by that kind of a story."

Jeff had no comment because he really only knew Morgan Scarbrough through stories. The man was almost legendary. All he could say was: "It probably wasn't that simple, Hyatt. I doubt like hell that Morgan Scarbrough could be talked into a bushwhack, too." He shrugged that aside; if it had happened, why then it had happened and standing out there all night talking about it wasn't going to make it seem any more plausible, furthermore, it wasn't Scarbrough being ambushed that really mattered; not to Jeff Stuart and the town of Duro, anyway.

"Have you told his brother?"

"Yeah. He leaned on the bars staring out at me and never said a lousy word."

"Probably can't believe it either. How about Henry, did you tell him?"

Sumner sighed. "That damned old fool, trying to get up a petition to force me to send Will Ray down to Nogales. *Of course* I'll send him down there. I don't need a damned paper signed by a lot of lily-livers to make me do that. I'm surprised at old Henry. I can remember, years back, some of the Apache hunts he was on. They used to say he was one of the cleverest and deadliest . . . Oh well; now he's an old man; I reckon that's made a difference."

"Pick up any other details?" asked Jeff. "How did the ambush come out?"

Sumner knew very little more. "The stage-driver got it off some drovers who'd been down at Cabral last night. They were on their way back over the line after a wild week. All they knew was that some *Rurales* ambushed some *gringos,* supposedly Texans, a dozen or so miles east of Cabral, shot the hell out of them and captured their leader. They said the Mexicans had identified Morgan Scarbrough as the *jefe.* The driver didn't know anything else; how many got killed or wounded." Sumner stepped over, settled his shoulders against the corral and concluded the recitation with a personal remark.

"All that really matters, I reckon, is that

Scarbrough didn't get the damned saddlebags, and the Mexicans got Scarbrough."

Jeff thought that was about right, then
Hyatt Sumner brought Jeff's thoughts back
from Mexico with his next remark.

"About Will Ray—I'll send a letter over
to Texas and see if they'll still pay the thousand dollars bounty it says they'll pay on
an old flyer I've got on him. Then I'll put in
a claim for you, and send him along for the
Federals to sweat about down at Nogales—
and life around here will get back to
normal, meanin' it'll start getting dull as
hell while we wait for hot weather to
come."

Hyatt smiled.

Jeff had not thought of a reward. He
probably should have since everyone who
rode with Morgan Scarbrough was notorious enough to be worth something,
somewhere, dead or alive.

About the only private thoughts he'd

had about the Scarbroughs had to do with personal misgivings about their success below the border. Evidently those misgivings had been vindicated. Otherwise, he had felt a vague, not-altogether creditable, uneasiness; he did not like the idea of being involved in anything that had to do with men like the Scarbroughs. He still did not like the idea, but at least now, with Will Ray Scarbrough in custody, and the other members of his band down in Mexico shot up, dead or also locked up, maybe there wasn't much to worry about.

Maybe.

He straightened up off the corral. "Care for a shot of lemon-juice and *tequila* on my patio, Hyatt?"

Sumner rolled up his eyes. "Hell; I thought you'd never ask."

Jeff laughed and led the way. The traditional way to drink *tequila* was to, first, pour a pinch of salt on the back of the hand, or in the enclosure beside the thumb when a fist was made, hold this up, toss off the breathtakingly fiery Mexican liquor, then quickly lick the salt.

That was how Marshal Sumner and Jeff Stuart had their drink on the patio. What made it even better, this time, was that Jeff had squeezed the juice from a fresh-picked lemon into the *tequila*. Lemons, which were a luxury elsewhere on the U.S. side of the border, actually were not as rare on the desert as one might have thought; in Mexico there were many places where people grew them, and sent them north in leather *alforjas,* two to a pack-mule.

Sumner drank, tongued off the salt, put down the small shot-glass and blew out a shaky breath. "That gawddamned stuff'd melt the hair right off a brass monkey," he gasped, then he smiled. "No wonder the greasers aren't much bothered by belly-worms." As he declined a refill and fished round through several pockets for his makings, he crossed to the bench, picked up one of the spurs lying there, and under the pretext of examining its intricate silver overlay and engraving, he said, "That's a mighty handsome girl—John Stedman's niece." He vigorously rubbed a thumb-pad over silver to bring on a light sheen so that he could trace out the engraving better. "I expect by now she's told you her folks were massacred by Cheyenne stronghearts in that Flint Hills wipe-out up in the Dakota Territory a while back."

Jeff, still holding his glass, watched the lawman's hat-shadowed, averted face. "Yeah, she told me, Hyatt. What are you getting at?"

Sumner raised his eyes. "Nothing, specially, Jeff. Well; maybe something. I'm about twenty years older'n you. When you're my age you'll understand this a lot better'n you'll understand it now, but you see, never having had a family, no daughter—or son either, for that matter—and having talked with Joyce a few times . . . knowing that she had one hell of a hurt up there in the north country . . ."

Jeff's unwavering stare finally brightened slightly with understanding. "She's got an uncle to worry about her, Hyatt."

Sumner put down the spur. "Yeah, I know."

"It's your job, Hyatt? You're warning me not to trifle around, and leanin' on the badge you wear to do it?"

"Oh hell no," exclaimed Marshal Sumner, loudly and exasperatedly. "You know a damned better'n that . . . Well; all right, I was sticking my damned big beak in where it don't belong. But like I tried to explain—I never had a daughter, but if I'd had one I'd expect her to look like that. Sort of leggy and thoroughbred-looking, with short, taffy hair and a nice wholesome attitude towards life."

Jeff leaned, put the glass down, then removed his hat and pitched it to the bench where his spurs were lying. This was something new to him. Not only in Marshal Sumner, but in anyone else. But there was another new emotion within him too, and between the pair of them he really did not know quite what to say. He did not feel that he had to justify anything he did, or had in mind doing, to Hyatt Sumner—nor anyone else, for the matter of that. But he truly believed that the marshal was wistfully serious, and in a way that was kind of sad. Maybe every man deserved a son and a daughter. Jeff was still some distance from knowing much about that, but he could at least get a glimpse of it, so, in the end, he said, "I gave her a sorrel horse this evening. I'm going to help her break it." He looked over at Sumner. "I've seen my share of 'em, Hyatt, but this one sure as hell isn't like any of the others."

Sumner went over to the gate without revealing what he thought, now. "See you in the morning, Jeff. By the way—know anyone who'd be interested in getting paid mileage for gun guarding Will Ray Scarbrough in chains down to Nogales on the stage?"

"Not by a damned sight I don't," Stuart replied. "See you tomorrow, Hyatt."

"Yeah. Thanks for the drink. Good night."

ELEVEN

STUNNING NEWS!

Joyce arrived at ten o'clock and when Jeff went out back he found her in the corral talking to the sorrel horse, which was the first he knew that she wasn't tending store with her uncle. She turned a quick, nice smile at him and with one hand lightly stroking the sorrel's neck, she said, "I think he likes me, Jeff."

There was a true answer to that, but Jeff did not offer it; no unbroke horse ever "liked" any two-legged creature. When they stood perfectly still allowing someone to stroke their neck it was an act of sufferance; the horse was not prepared to fight, and the person's touch really wasn't something that hurt or angered them, so they would simply stand perfectly still waiting for the two-legged creature to have done with it, and go away.

Jeff entered the corral but stayed back. *Two* people made any un-handled horse nervous. He waited for her to ease her hand to the horse's head, knowing exactly what would happen, but he said nothing until she reached, and the horse snorted then ducked away. As she turned, a little chagrined, a little bewildered, he smiled.

"Even broke horses would just as soon you'd pet them somewhere besides on the face. Give him time. You did one thing right anyway; never approach a horse you don't know, directly in front. Always walk slightly to one side. That's in case he takes a notion to strike. If you're not squarely in front, chances are he won't hit you. And remember this; a kicking horse knocks you *away* from him, but a striking horse lashes out with a front foot, and if he catches you, he'll pull you *to* him, probably *under* him, and that's when he'll step on you and maybe bust something."

She frowned across the corral at Jeff. "Didn't you say you'd help me with him?"

He laughed at her expression. "I *am* helping you. I don't want anything to happen to you."

"You're scaring me," she said tartly, and twisted for a look at the sorrel, who had edged over where his friends were and was peering out at her from the protection of the other horses. Then she turned and walked back to Jeff near the corral gate.

"I thought, all you had to do was let him know you were his friend," she complained. "Then he'd trust you."

"Give him time, Joyce. Give *any* horse time. The only thing a horse can figure out fast, is when to be frightened—then he can move so quick you'll be sitting on the ground before you even know something's spooked him."

She leaned with the golden sunlight

upon her face and throat, and tangled in her taffy hair, her face faintly marred by a doubtful frown. "How long does it take to break one to saddle?" she asked, still gazing at the sorrel.

He grinned to himself. "To break a horse to ride—just to sit atop of and rein around—doesn't take very long. Few weeks maybe, depending upon the horse. That particular one will break easy. But to break a horse to rope off of, or to cut cattle, or to run mustangs, takes about a year of damned hard work." He turned towards her. She was profiled to him full length, and except for the large-orange thrust of breasts, she was lithe and boyish, with small hands and feet. "I'll get a halter and a sack from the barn," he said, reaching round to open the gate.

She faced him. "A sack?"

He stepped out through the gate without explaining. "I'll show you. While

I'm in the barn talk your way up and pet him again."

He went to the barn, picked up one of the sacks that had covered Will Ray Scarbrough's saddle—which was still lying there while its owner was in the jailhouse—got a halter off a wall-peg, and returned to the corral.

She had got half-way to the sorrel, but now, as the other horses eased away, so did the sorrel. Jeff went over to her, handed her the empty sack, told her to stand still, and manoeuvred his way around until he had the sorrel cornered. Then he haltered the animal, talked quietly to it, and led it back where she was. Then he handed her the shank, took the sack, and began slowly and very gently rubbing the horse's neck, withers, back and shoulders. At first, the sorrel offered to suck sideways to avoid the sack. He didn't snort but he rolled his eyes as though he might snort.

They worked more than an hour. Jeff had "sacked out" the sorrel all over, even around the rump and up his neck to the poll. The sorrel eventually adopted his earlier attitude of patient waiting; he knew now that the sack would not hurt him, so all he wanted was for the man to get it over with.

Jeff handed the sack to Joyce. "Slow," he told her. "Very slow and very gentle, and keep your free hand on him at all times, so that if he jumps away, you've got something to push yourself away with. He's not going to deliberately hurt you, but take my word for it, a broken toe is just as painful on purpose or by accident. And keep talking to him."

Some people had the knack of handling unbroken horses, some did not have it and could never develop it. She had it. He held the shank and waited until she had worked her way gently completely around the horse. He offered only one admonition, and that was when she was near his flank.

"When you walk behind a horse either brush very close, so that if he happens to kick he'll hit you with his hocks, not his hoofs, and can't hurt you, or else stay eight feet out so that he can't reach you at all."

He expected her to do the obvious, to walk far out, which commonsense indicated was the safest way. She didn't, she kept talking, slowly moving, kept one hand upon the horse's hips, and kept the sack moving. Then she leaned close and eased around to the far side. The sorrel turned his head just enough to watch, and of course if she had suddenly tripped, or had done anything suddenly, he would have tucked-tail and jumped ahead, but she glided around without mishap and continued sacking him all the way up the off-side.

That was enough for one day. Jeff

removed the halter, told her to stand perfectly still, and when the sorrel figured out
that he was free, finally, he took a couple of
tentative steps, then walked quietly away
from them.

Jeff looked across. "First lesson," he
said. "Come along, it's getting hot out
here."

He took her to the barn, where they left
the halter and sack, then he took her across
to his patio where it was usually about ten
degrees cooler than the back-lot was.

She went over to smell the citrus blos-
soms, then turned slowly in fig-tree shade
and watched him get comfortable over on
the wooden bench in the shade. She said,
"Will you explain something to me, Jeff?"

He thought he knew what the question
would be. "Maybe; if it's about horses—
I've been around them all my life. I've had
more horses for friends than I've had
people."

"Not that."

He nodded. "Yeah; I didn't think it was. About last night at the gate?"

"Yes."

He removed his hat and leaned back with his shoulders against the cool adobe wall at his back. "Well . . . do I have to explain it, right now?"

"Don't you want to?"

He kept gazing at her. She was indeed different. Hyatt Sumner had hit upon the right word: Wholesome. She was waiting and he didn't know exactly how to tell her about the interlude last night. "I want to, sure, Joyce, only—next week would be a better time."

"What's next week got to do with it?"

He sighed, "You're stubborn."

She smiled and strolled over to sit near him. "Not really but I'm a woman, and women are naturally curious. It had a significance for you; I figured that out last

night while I was lying in bed thinking back
. . . I've been wondering about it ever
since." She leaned back beside him. "All
right—next week." Then she abruptly
changed the subject. "Some freighters who
brought a load to the back-door this
morning were telling my uncle about
Morgan Scarbrough being caught down in
Mexico." She looked at him. "I talked with
Marshal Sumner this morning, Jeff."

"Yeah," he said, feeling the first faint
stirrings of annoyance with Hyatt Sumner.
"And he told you why I went down there a
few days back."

"Yes."

"Well; so much for that."

She slowly shook her head at him. "No."

He straightened on the bench. "What
do you mean—no?"

"The freighters told my uncle that
Morgan Scarbrough ransomed himself."

"*What!*"

"That's what they said. That Morgan Scarbrough paid a big ransom to the Mexicans to let him go, and they did it. He, and four of his men, all that survived being ambushed by the Mexicans."

Jeff let all his breath out, slowly, then rummaged for his makings and went to work to frowningly roll and light a cigarette. *This* was something that had never once crossed his mind as a possibility, and yet maybe it should have; the Mexicans would do that occasionally, providing they got enough money out of it. But *Morgan Scarbrough?* He was worth a fortune in rewards; if the Mexicans had known that, which the *Rurales* most certainly would have, since they were lean, human wolves when it came to collaring *gringo* fugitives whom they sold back to U.S. officials as often as they could, why then the other answer as to why they hadn't done it this time had to be that Scarbrough had paid the Mexicans much more for *not* handing him over, and for turning him loose, than the Mexicans could have got any other way.

"Jeff . . . ?"

He leaned back again. "Yes?"

"My uncle believes he'll come up here looking for his brother."

There was not much doubt about *that*; every story Jeff had ever heard about the Scarbroughs said something about their fierce loyalty. He stood up. "I'll walk you back to the store." He turned, offering his hands. She reached, took them both and came up off the bench directly in front of him. For one bad moment he forgot completely about the Scarbroughs. She may have too, because she stood no more than six or eight inches from him, still holding hands, looking up into his face—scarcely breathing. Then she stepped sideways swiftly and kept her face averted while he recovered, leaned to pick up his hat, and as they walked towards the gate, she said, "Jeff? My uncle says Marshal Sumner has to get rid of Will Ray Scarbrough right away."

He held the gate then walked out after her. There was no doubt about that, either. "I'll go talk to him," he told her, as they moved across in the direction of the roadway.

They were both intent upon their private thoughts all the way down to the store, where he left her and hiked across to Hyatt Sumner's office. She stood back in the store's pleasant, spice-scented gloom and watched him, then her uncle came forward, also squinted over across the road, and said. "Did you tell him what those freighters said?"

She nodded. "Yes. It upset him."

John Stedman commented about that wryly. "I wouldn't be surprised. It upset me too. He's entering Sumner's building."

Joyce turned, as Jeff disappeared from sight over across the road. "He didn't say so, but I think he's going to tell the marshal they have to get rid of their prisoner."

John Stedman fondled a big gold watch-chain that was draped across his ample middle. "They'd *better* get rid of him," he grumbled, heading back for one of the counters. "And they'd also better let his brother know he's not here in Duro."

Joyce, leaning upon the table in the dry-goods section, looking solemn, said, "Uncle John, the next stage doesn't get here until late this afternoon, does it?"

"No. There are only two coaches through daily, one in the morning, one in the . . . What are you thinking?"

"I was thinking—how long would it take Morgan Scarbrough to get up here if he was released by the Mexicans yesterday? Couldn't he be close to Duro right now?"

John Stedman rubbed his palms

together and did some quiet calculating. "He could have been here about dawn, if he'd ridden straight through; and if he's wise about travelling the desert country, he would have made the crossing last night."

Joyce straightened up. "If they can't send his brother down to Nogales until evening . . . ?"

Stedman stared at his niece. "Yes. I see your point. It would be too late, wouldn't it—unless they send an armed guard on the stage, too."

"Not you, Uncle, and not Jeff," Joyce exclaimed hurriedly.

TWELVE

AN OLD MAN'S IRE

Jeff was saying almost the same thing to Hyatt Sumner over in the marshal's small office. "Not John Stedman, Hyatt, and I've already done my part in this. Which reminds me, you haven't mentioned that damned amnesty since I got back."

Sumner, drinking coffee at his desk when Jeff had walked in, finished the coffee now and went to rinse his crockery cup in a water-bucket before hanging it from a nail behind his small Franklyn stove. "I thought I'd told you; I wrote up the petition for pardon, along with a cover-letter to the commandant down at Nogales for him to add his approval, and forward the damned thing to Washington. It'll take time. I've never yet done anything that wasn't routine where the government was concerned, that it didn't seem to take forever."

Jeff went over and sat down. "Yeah. Put that on my headstone."

Hyatt turned. "You're taking this bad. What the hell, *I'm* the one Morgan'll be after, not you."

Jeff raised sceptical eyes. "Who brought him in and handed him over?"

Marshal Sumner didn't believe that was much of a factor. "Morgan's going to want him released. He's not going to spend much time trying to rattle *your* cage. He dassn't; I've sent word down to Nogales about the rumour those damned freighters spread all over town. The army down there will sure as hell put out patrols all along the border."

"What the hell good will that do?" demanded Jeff. "If the Mexicans turned him loose yesterday or the night before, he's been across the border for at least ten hours. Patrolling the border now is like locking the barn after the horse has been stolen. What we need up around Duro, right now, is a couple of those patrols that are wandering around down there on the border."

"Calm down," grumbled the lawman. "I also told Nogales that. As long as we've got Will Ray here in Duro, we're going to need protection."

Jeff pushed his hat to the back of his head and watched Hyatt Sumner amble back to his desk and sit down. "We got to get him out of here, Hyatt."

Sumner pressed his fingertips together. "The coach won't even reach town until—"

"I don't mean by the damned stage," exclaimed Jeff. "We got to put irons on him and get him out of town in a wagon or astride a horse."

Marshal Sumner looked shocked.

"What the hell are you talking about?"

"Let Morgan hang down there on the desert somewhere and waylay the coach. His brother won't be on it. We'll slip him out of town this evening after dark, and we'll take him due south, like we're heading straight for the border—which they won't be expecting. Then we'll turn east and ride hell-for-leather for Nogales."

Marshal Sumner's shock passed. He got a look of pained exasperation upon his face next. "Jeff, damn it all, as far as we know right this minute, Morgan Scarbrough doesn't even know we've *got* his brother." Sumner leaned back expansively. "He was in some lousy Mex *calabozo* down around Cabral when we picked up Will Ray. Until he scouts up this here town he's not going to know for sure where his brother is."

Jeff gently shook his head. "Hyatt, you're forgetting something. You and I knew for a fact that only the pair of us knew I was taking those damned saddle-bags over the line a few nights back. And we were wrong as all hell, weren't we?"

Sumner stared in silence for a moment, then he scowled and prepared to speak, but something intruded to change his mind.

In the end all he did was arise from behind the desk and start back for the coffee pot, but at that moment the roadside door opened and the gunsmith walked in, still wearing his oily old canvas apron. Both Sumner and Jeff Stuart glanced around.

Henry Steele shook a finger at the lawman. "Hyatt, I *knew* you'd ought to get rid of that bastard last night. I knew it as well as I know my own lousy name. And now what?"

Jeff wanted to smile for the first time since Joyce had told him about those freighters talking to her uncle. Old Steele was stiff with outrage; it was as though this entire travail were the fault of the U.S.

deputy marshal.

Sumner finished filling his cup for the second time before turning back, with a resigned look, and saying, "Gawddammit, Henry, why don't you just stick to fixing guns?"

"Because I'm a citizen of this here town," screeched the old man, stung to a fresh outburst by the lawman's attitude, "and every last one of us got a right to lawful protection. And here you are, drinkin' coffee while there's a whole passel of them *pistoleros*, maybe fifteen, twenty of 'em, heading for Duro as sure as—"

"Four," said Sumner. "Four outlaws and Morgan Scarbrough. That's all the freighters said lived through the ambush and fight down below Cabral. Not fifteen or twenty."

"Five then," exclaimed the agitated old man. "Hyatt, I've *been* there; I'm standing right here to tell you that four like them boys, *plus* Morgan Scarbrough, is equal to twenty or fifty ordinary *pistoleros* . . . And you're drinkin' coffee, gawddammit!"

Jeff finally did smile. "Henry, take it easy."

The gunsmith turned stiffly and glared down where Jeff was sitting. "Yeah," he snorted. "And you, Jeff Stuart—you had to catch that bastard, didn't you? Whyn't you just give him a horse and send him on his way? You know what you done; you put this whole damned town in real peril. That's what you done. When I was a young buck we used some understandin' of situations; we didn't always string 'em up to the first handy tree, sometimes it was a heap smarter to sort of look the other way and leave a bridled horse standin' close by so's they could make a break for it."

Hyatt Sumner did not touch his coffee. He leaned back, rolled up his eyes, and waited out the storm.

"Now I'll tell you what's got to be done," went on the indignant gunsmith. "We got to organise the town, first off. We got to have armed men on patrol day an' night until this damned mess is over. And we got to send Will Ray Scarbrough down to Nogales on the night coach. Then we got to get word to his brother, some way or other, that we don't have him in Duro no more."

Jeff looked amusedly over at Marshal Sumner, but the lawman was not even looking down yet. Jeff turned casually back to the gunsmith. "Henry; you want to bring along your buffler rifle and ride down to Nogales with me tonight, while I take Will Ray down there?"

Old Steele's mouth fell open. "You're crazy," he gasped. "You're talkin' like a crazy man, Jeff."

Stuart did not resist that suggestion. "I was crazy to ever listen to Hyatt in the first place, but that's water under the bridge now. Henry; I'll bet you eight good horses . . . no, I gave one away . . . I'll bet you seven good horses that Morgan Scarbrough already knows we have his brother in our jailhouse right here in Duro."

"All right," conceded the old man, bobbing his head like a bird. "Sure he knows; fellers like Morgan Scarbrough's got eyes in the backs of their heads and they always got more'n one ear to the ground."

"Well then, Henry," went on Jeff, "we can't send his brother south on the night stage, can we?"

"The hell we can't! Why not?"

"Because Scarbrough wouldn't just take his brother off the damned stage, Henry, which we don't want, after catching Will Ray, but Morgan would also kill the whip and the guard—and anyone from town who rode along. We're not going to let that happen."

The gunsmith's entire attitude changed. He went to a chair, sank down, and muttered, "Oh gawddamn." Then he recovered a little and pierced Jeff with a snake-bright stare. "I'm too old, Jeff. I'm just an old man who's been tryin' to hang on at his trade until the Good Lord beckons."

Jeff's grin firmed up again. "Leave the Good Lord out of it, Henry. This will be just you, me, and Will Ray Scarbrough. There's a fair moon tonight. If we push right along we can make Nogales before sunup. Bring along your canteen, some jerky in case you get hungry, plenty of slugs for your rifle, and a shell-belt with a Colt."

"I don't have a horse no more, Jeff."

"You can use mine," said Marshal Sumner.

Steele glared, suddenly angry all over again at the lawman. "Dang your hide anyway. Hyatt Sumner! You think this is funny, don't you? Well, let me tell you something, this here is *your* job, not mine. You're the legal law around here!"

"Who'll be in town in case Scarbrough doesn't wait for the stage?" asked Jeff, and shook his head at the gunsmith. "You and I'll take Will Ray down to Nogales, and Hyatt will organise a vigilance committee here in town to mind things until we get back sometime tomorrow."

Hyatt Sumner arose and looked at the pair of men in front of his desk. "There's one thing: It occurred to me about an hour ago, before either one of you showed up. If Morgan got up around here sometime last night, or maybe early this morning, and if he knows we've got Will Ray in our *calabozo* here in town—you can bet a new saddle-blanket that he's got someone sitting out there watching this damned jailhouse like the devil watching a crippled saint."

Jeff shrugged. "We won't ride out until

after nightfall."

Sumner smiled without humour. "There's a right nice moon, tonight, Jeff remember?"

Old Henry Steele, who had been following this exchange, suddenly threw himself back into his chair. and groaned loudly.

Jeff pushed his legs out their full length, crossed them at the ankles, and studied the row of vicious faces across the room upon the wall where Marshal Sumner tacked up his most recent wanted flyers. The Scarbroughs were not over there, but the men who *were* over there probably had the same thoroughly malevolent look on their faces. Jeff knew for a fact that Will Ray Scarbrough would murder him with a gun, knife, length of chain, or just a handy rock, if he could get the chance.

"We'll just have to take a chance on that moon not being up when we sneak out of town," he told Sumner and old Steele.

"Henry . . . ?"

"I'm not going to do it. Jeff, for Chriz' sake, I'm too old and stiff and measly for something like that. What you need is a younger man," Old Steele glared. "*Him*, for instance; him with that fancy circled-star on his shirtfront. He gets paid good money for puttin' his life on the line. And anyway, my eyes aren't as good as they once was. If there's trouble, me being an old, rattle-brained feller, for all you know I could up and shoot the wrong man. Maybe I'd even shoot *you*, son. Now you know don't neither one of us want nothing like that to—"

"Wait a minute," broke in Jeff, and shot a narrowed look at Hyatt Sumner. "Isn't there a reward on Morgan Scarbrough?"

Sumner reared up. "A reward! Why hell, they'd give you half Texas and all the money in it, if you nailed Morgan Scarbrough." Sumner leaned to rifle through some papers atop his desk. "I calculated it last night. Well; I can't ever find anything on this damned desk, but I tallied up the rewards and they came to something like five thousand dollars."

Old Henry Steele sat in stunned silence, his faded, bright old eyes fixed stonily to Marshal Sumner's face. He said, "Hyatt; how much did you say that was?"

"Five thousand or more, Henry, as near as I recollect. I've got that scrap of paper here somewhere."

"Never mind the damned scrap of paper," said the gunsmith, arising slowly from his chair. "Five thousand . . . but hell, Jeff, we probably won't see no sign of Morgan. The idea'll be to skulk round and *not* see him, won't it?"

"Well, yes," conceded Stuart. "But if he's looking for Will Ray, Henry, you can damned well bet *he's* going to be doing some skulking around too. And I remember from the war that Morgan Scarbrough had a reputation, especially among the blue-bellies—excuse me, Hyatt—especially among the Yankees, for being one hell of a skulker." Jeff stood up too. "Henry, you're a gambling man at heart. Tell me: Would you gamble five thousand that we *might* find him in the dark, tonight?"

Old Steele's bright, pale eyes narrowed. "Sonny, forty years back I done my best skulkin' in the dark—and that was only for twelve dollars a month. What time you figure to start out?"

THIRTEEN

A VOICE OF DISSENT

After Henry departed Marshal Sumner put a cynical gaze upon Jeff Stuart. "And I thought *John Stedman* was a salesman," he said quietly. "You ought to be ashamed of yourself. Him an old man and all."

"Yeah," stated Jeff. "*And* a damned gossip, *and* a guy who runs around stirring folks up. Hyatt, as long as he thinks we might come into the money for Morgan Scarbrough, he's going to keep his damned mouth shut, and *that* is what I got to thinking about when he was making all that fight-talk when he first walked in here. There'd be no way to keep him quiet—unless we came up with something that smelled like money. Old Henry's as avaricious as—"

"*We,*" exclaimed the lawman. "*We* didn't come up with anything. *You* did." Sumner studied the younger man. "And you sure changed your mind in a hurry. When you first came in here you weren't going to touch Will Ray with a forty foot pole. Now, you're going to sneak him down to Nogales."

"*Try* to sneak him down to Nogales," said Jeff, correcting the lawman. "And the reason I changed was because if *I* hadn't decided to take Will Ray, who would have?"

"Well . . ."

"Yeah, I know," stated Jeff dryly. "John Stedman or one of the fellers who hang around the liverybarn or the blacksmith shop." Jeff stood up. He stepped to the door. "Have Will Ray handy when I come back after nightfall, Hyatt." He walked back out of the marshal's office, considered the sunlighted front of the east-side stores over across the way, and decided he had more than half a day yet to kill.

He ambled on back up to his corral-yard, went almost indifferently over to glance in at the Sanchez-horses—and one of them was not there. The fine-boned sorrel was not in the corral. He looked, waved his arms to make the other seven animals string out so that he could be absolutely sure, then his heart got a feeling as though a steel wire were snugged up around it.

What in the hell would possess her to think she could ride that damned horse; he had *told* her and *told* her . . . He stepped riskly over to the barn entrance, with some vague thought in mind of saddling the seal-brown to go look for her.

She was in the cool shade with the sorrel haltered and cross-tied, brushing him with firm, long strokes, and talking to him. She saw Jeff across the horse's back, but the horse did not see him, not right away because he had his head down, his lower lip hanging, and his eyes half closed in complete comfort. Only when Jeff spoke did the horse widen one eye and watch him, and that, of course, kept Jeff from using the tone of voice he wanted to use. It also kept him from marching in there, up close.

From back by the door, in a quiet, green-colt-tone-of-voice, he said, "You liked to scairt the daylights out of me. He wasn't in the corral. I thought you might have gone and tried to ride him."

Joyce looked across the intervening distance with liquid-soft gunmetal eyes. "I wouldn't attempt that, not without you being around. Anyway, you told me not to rush things. I just wanted him to get to know me. So we came in here, because it was hot in the corral, and now we're getting along wonderfully."

There was no denying that. The horse

was as relaxed as an animal could get, without falling down. Jeff leaned in the doorway watching her. She had a knack with animals; maybe she knew it, maybe she didn't know it, but not everyone had a natural way with critters . . . She also looked very alluring, in his barn, her taffy hair loose and in heavy coils around her face, her lean, lithe body tantalisingly supple when she moved. He blew out a breath, fished for his makings and went to work on a smoke. She watched him covertly, and right after he had lit up she said, "Jeff . . . you're going to try and get Morgan Scarbrough's brother down to Nogales, aren't you?"

He gave her a hard look. "What makes you think so—or have you been talking to someone?"

"No. I haven't spoken to anyone. I just think . . . that I know you that well. You're going to try it, aren't you?"

He smiled crookedly. "It's a big secret."

She leaned upon the sorrel with both arms across his back. "Please let someone else do it."

"Who?" he asked.

"Well; I don't know, but there's surely someone else. Maybe even three or four other men around Duro who would do it."

He gave her that crooked, mirthless smile again. "Knowing Morgan Scarbrough's out there somewhere? Don't bet any money there's someone else. Anyway, I know this country a hell of a lot better than either of the Scarbroughs, or anyone who is riding with them." It suddenly hit him, how she had said that, *"Please let someone else do it,"* as though it were important to her that nothing should happen to him.

He dwelt upon this lingeringly—then common sense came to suggest that she would be that solicitous about anyone, and that half-spoiled the entire thrill of the thing for him.

He walked in, slowly, and passed around to the far side of the sorrel where she was. "Don't worry about it. Morgan Scarbrough may have been one of the best guerrillas back during the war, but this isn't like it was then. Not at all."

She turned, facing him. "Isn't it? Don't bullets still kill people?"

He sighed. Arguing with her was like trying to talk sense into a spoiled horse. Instead of carrying on this conversation he went over, got one of the sacks, brought it back and handed it to her. "Every day," he said. "The brush and currycomb are fine, but the sack means more. About next week, you see, you'll substitute a saddle-blanket for the sack."

She took the sack from him but kept watching his face. Nor did she turn back towards the horse. Finally, she stepped completely away from the horse. "Jeff . . .

suppose something happens to you?"

"Nothing is—"

"Suppose," she interjected. "Just *suppose* it does."

He fidgeted, killed his cigarette under a booted foot and raised his eyes slowly. "I'll come back," he said softly. "I'll tell you something—I've got the best reason a man ever had to come back."

They regarded one another for a moment, then she moved completely away from the horse, put the sack back where he had got it, from that pile over where Will Ray Scarbrough's saddle and bridle still lay, then she went resolutely over, took his hand and tugged him towards the rear barn opening, back where the shade was beginning to fan out, now that the sun was off-centre in its flawless, faded blue sky.

She dropped his hand and swung to face him. "Do you know what the law of averages is?"

He saw the resolute set to her jaw and the dead-level gunmetal eyes, and almost smiled. She impressed him, now, like a mother scolding a child. "Sure, I know what it is. You ride enough bucking horses and someday you're going to get hurt."

She showed fire and exasperation when she retorted. "No! You went down to Mexico. You delivered the plunder, and by luck, you made it both ways without a scratch. Jeff; the law of averages says that if you keep doing things like this . . . Why can't Marshal Sumner go instead of you?"

Maybe Marshal Sumner could go. Something had been said about this. He looked steadily back at her. "Because, Joyce, I volunteered to go." He started to turn away. She stepped closer to force him to face her. He stopped moving. They were both slightly upset and breathless. Without being fully aware, he reached out, and she came up inside his arms, and out front someone coughed, then was seized by a regular fit of coughing.

They sprang apart as though suddenly a rattlesnake had dropped between them.

Jeff twisted to see who was out there, but no one was visible from the rear doorway, so he strolled ahead the full distance. An old Mexican, hat in hand, was standing impassively to one side of the doorway; of course he had seen them at the back of the barn, but to look at him now one would believe he was surprised when Jeff stepped forth.

He smiled. His Spanish was border-Mex, but that was all anyone spoke, and if anyone had tried to use it in a place like Veracruz or Mexico City, he would have drawn blank stares, but without hesitation the old man said, "Mister, I am here for you with a message. Friend, I was last night at the house of Eusebio Sanchez to whom I confess to be a relation. The message, mister, is not for you to rest tranquil, for there are five pistol-men who want you. Know then, friend, that these men believe you put the brother of one into the jail-house. A cowboy from Duro said this was so. My relation thinks that right now for you a great distance would be a healthy thing." The old Mexican's smile wavered. He cleared his throat, raised one hand with all fingers and the thumb stiff as nails, and said, "*Cinco*." He cleared his throat again. "Five."

Jeff nodded. In Spanish he asked when the *pistoleros* left Cabral. The old Mexican only shrugged. "Sometime," he stated in English, and clapped the hat back upon his head as though to depart. Jeff held up a hand. "One moment, my friend. Who was the cowboy from Duro who told these men I took this other outlaw to the jailhouse?"

The old man flopped his arms. "I do not know, Mister. I only can say what my relation Eusebio Sanchez told me." He looked steadily at Jeff with patient, black eyes. "I have done what I said I would do."

Jeff nodded, dug, rounded up a silver cartwheel from the silver in a trouser pocket and put it into the old man's hand. The Mexican protested; ritual and good manners required no less. Jeff insisted. The old man pitched up his shoulders and let them fall. He was, he said, ashamed to take money for a simple thing like perhaps saving another man's life, still, if the horseman wished things to be this way, then he could rest quietly in the absolute knowledge that the old man would this very evening buy a taper and set it in place over in Mex-town's mission.

Jeff watched the old man shuffle back in the direction of the roadway, and turned only when Joyce came soundlessly out to him. He did not have to ask what she had heard, it was written all over her face.

He said, "Come along, we're going to take you back to the store." When she stepped away he thought she meant to go take care of the sorrel horse. "Never mind that," he told her. "I'll turn the damned horse out later. Come along."

She remained in position. "Jeff; I understood what he said."

Stuart smiled. "I reckon everyone understands border-Spanish. It's about as complicated as pig-latin." He reached for her hand. "Joyce, I've got enough problems."

She yielded, when he said that, but as they were passing around the side of the house she had a suggestion. "Take five men with you. Four at the very least. That'll even the odds."

"Yeah, and it'll also make enough noise to be heard a country mile."

She said no more. Neither of them noticed a few people upon the sidewalks on both sides of the roadway gazing frankly over as the lithe, supple girl and the stocky, powerful man crossed the roadway and walked silently side by side down as far as the general store. There, he paused a moment to look at her.

"I'm going to have a hell of a time concentrating on the Scarbroughs tonight." He smiled gently. "I'm going to be wondering and worrying about what would have happened if that old Mex hadn't arrived."

She did not blush nor lower her eyes. "I'll be at the barn tomorrow evening. If you don't get back by then, I'll be there day after tomorrow. I'll be there every day from now until you *do* come back . . . And there won't be any old man the next time." She turned and moved swiftly into the store.

He crossed the road without even looking at the marshal's office—where a tanned, thoughtful face was framed in the window—walked all the way back home, and went inside to change his clothing, to check his weapons, to eat a big meal, drink a bottle of *cerbeza* with sediment in the bottom of the bottle, and finally, to go out back and sit in peace and solitude, and slowly falling shadows, waiting until night-fall came.

He did *not* want to do what he had said he would do. He could think of a dozen very good reasons for not doing it. Some of them were so entirely plausible that he almost believed them himself. But of course he would do it, because he had said he would.

If his choice of a companion was a little incongruous, he did not think so. Whatever else old Henry Steele was, no one could deny that, aged now or not, he was the wiry, wizened, knowledgeable kind of a man to ride the night time desert on this kind of an undertaking with.

FOURTEEN

TAKING THE LONG CHANCE

John Stedman was with Marshal Sumner after nightfall. He had the look of a man to whom some distasteful variety of interruption had arrived in his personal life. He did not say it, but his expression indicated that he was now, for the second time lately, feeling both resentful and resigned about a coercive interlude which had compelled him to depart from his lifelong and comfortable habits.

John was a man of habit; he knew it and he liked it.

When Marshal Sumner said, "I think he'll make it all right," Stedman's pained expression deepened. " 'Maybe' isn't good enough, Hyatt. Futhermore my niece may be correct about the foolishness of him trying it alone."

"Henry will be with him."

Stedman made a face. "An old man who is in his seventies."

Hyatt Sumner's reply was terse. "John; if I had to go gallivanting out there in the night, I'd prefer Henry to anyone else around Duro." Sumner looked at his watch, stepped to the window and peered up at the sky, then he returned to the front of the desk where he had been leaning. "I understand your concern."

John looked over. "Do you?"

"Sure I do. I watched them walking from his place down to the store today. Then I saw him walk back, and the way she looked after him." Hyatt attempted a weak bluffness. "Make a right striking pair too, and I figure she could have done a heap worse."

John Stedman may have resented this intimacy because he did not relent in his pained look as he said, "Hyatt, she's been through two burials lately. It took her nigh a year to come back from them. She's taken an uncommon shine to Jeff Stuart," Stedman solemnly shook his head, "I don't want her to have to go through anything like that again . . . Hyatt, find four or five local cowboys or horse-hunters, and I'll personally pay each of them a hundred dollars to deliver Will Ray Scarbrough down to Nogales."

"Not a chance," replied the lawman. "It's too late in the day, but even if it wasn't the minute they heard who is waiting out there for someone to take Will Ray out of the *calabozo* . . ." Hyatt did not finish it; he did not have to.

This desultory discussion might have gone on longer except that Henry Steele arrived, but out in the back alley with a dark horse saddled, bridled, and rigged out with a Winchester boot, a small roll behind the cantle, and a blanket-cloth covered metal canteen at the swells.

Henry refused to come inside, saying he would prefer to wait out back, and that when Jeff arrived, Henry would meet him in the alleyway; meanwhile, he'd tie his horse and do a little wandering around.

Marshal Sumner closed the door, went back to his front office and met John Stedman at the door. Stedman said, "I've got to be getting along." He stared at the lawman. "How many people know what you're going to try to do tonight?"

Hyatt was hopeful about that. "Henry Steele and Jeff, you and me. That's all."

Stedman said, "That's too many." He seemed to be ticking off names in his mind, hand resting upon the door-knob. Finally he said, "Henry . . . ?"

Hyatt shook his head. "He's got a gossip, John, but he's not a plain damned fool, and that's what he'd have to be to spill his guts about what's going on tonight, since he's smack-dab in the centre of it."

Stedman did not act entirely convinced before he left, and Hyatt Sumner didn't care whether Stedman was convinced or not; *he* felt fairly certain the secret would be well kept. He hoped very fervently it would be, but whether it was or not, like every man whose back was figuratively to the wall, he had explored a lot of options, and the one he was relying upon, now, more than any other, was the one he explained to Jeff, when Stuart came along after nightfall, and it had nothing much to do with anything he had previously discussed with either John Stedman or Henry Steele.

"You know the desert, Jeff. You probably know it better than most of the greasers over in Mex-town, and if Morgan figures he needs a scout, my guess is that that's where he'd go to hire one. I'm not much worried about what might happen once you're on your way. What keeps my guts in a knot is what happens between the time I go get Will Ray, and the time the three of you get out there. Morgan's going to be fig-urin' about like this too, I think. The best way to hit the enemy in strange country is when he's bunched up, unsuspecting, and just riding out."

Jeff laughed. "You Yankees always did worry a lot, Hyatt."

Sumner defended his premise. "Well, that happens to be the most crucial time—after you leave town and before you can get very far out on the desert."

Jeff did not argue about this. "All right. Just how much territory around town can five men cover? They sure as hell can't sur-round the town, can they?"

"They can watch the roads and trails, and they can—"

"Just fetch Will Ray, Hyatt," said Jeff,

beginning to feel slightly aggravated. "Where the hell is Henry?"

"In the back alley. All right, I'll get Will Ray. Incidentally, since Henry isn't using my horse, why don't you saddle him up for Will Ray?"

Jeff nodded about this suggestion, and when Marshal Sumner strode to the door, on his way over to get the prisoner, Jeff dug out a big gold watch, flipped open the case, studied the hands, pursed his lips in thoughtful concentration for a moment, then hiked on through to the back alley. He did not find Henry right away, although he found the dark horse with Henry's old rig on it. He waited a few minutes, until Henry glided out of the westerly night, then he scowled at the old man.

"Never mind scouting for 'Paches, damn it, Henry, you stay close," he growled at the old man. "Go up to my place, stay in the barn, and when I come along with

Scarbrough, you go out the back way, open the rear gate of the corral and chouse those horses loose—all but the sorrel horse. Don't make a lot of noise, just set those horses to stampeding across the desert the minute you see Will Ray and me ride into the yard. You understand that?"

"Sure, but what's the idea?"

"Just do as I say. And Henry, the moment you've got those horses scattered, get astride and hurry over where Will Ray and I'll be waiting. All clear?"

Steele nodded in the alleyway darkness. He did not frame another question, either. Instead of being his customary garrulous self, Henry stood straighter, moved quicker, and acted at least twenty years younger. Jeff noticed, and on his way back through to the front of the marshal's little building, he was tempted to grin to himself. Five thousand dollars was evidently one hell of an incentive to old Henry.

Hyatt Sumner returned from next door with Will Ray. Scarbrough, manacled, unshaven and malevolent-looking stared stonily at Jeff, who only glanced his way, then spoke aside to Hyatt Sumner. "How about rigging out your horse and tying him round back, Hyatt?"

Sumner departed without a word. Will Ray shook his head very slowly at Jeff. "You'll never bring it off. Not in God's green world. By now my brother's out there, settin' and waitin' and honing his Bowie knife to cut your lousy gullet."

Jeff made a cigarette, started to lip it, hesitated, and offered it to the outlaw. Will Ray leaned to accept. He could not raise his arms because a small chain from the manacles went round under his belt. As he sucked in smoke from Jeff's match, he stared with steady deadliness. Afterwards he said, "Give it up and get the hell out of the way, Stuart."

Jeff rolled a smoke without commenting. He finally said, "Listen to me, Will Ray, and damn you listen good; if you raise a yell or make any kind of a noise—I'll kill you."

They looked at one another. Will Ray then went back and sat down, eyes narrowed against curling smoke. "Tell me something, Stuart; was you in the war?"

"Yeah."

"Then that talk about a pardon from the government wasn't no lie."

Jeff smiled. "I don't lie, Will Ray. Not to you nor to anyone else. I don't figure I have to lie. Now you remember what I told you: When we ride out of here, don't do anything wrong. I wasn't bluffing about killing you."

Will Ray sighed. "You'll never make it."

Jeff was interested in Scarbrough's attitude. "What makes you think your brother's out there?"

"Why shouldn't he be?"

"Because the Mexicans caught him, shot him up in an ambush, and jugged him."

Will Ray inhaled, exhaled, and never once let his eyes wander from Jeff's face while he digested this information. "But he's out now, isn't he?"

Jeff nodded. "Yeah."

Will Ray's wide, thin lips curled. "Naturally. You see, Stuart, when Morg goes into a campaign he figures what he calls . . . all the contingencies. We been having brushes with greasers since the war. Morg says there never was a Messican born you couldn't buy. He keeps a war-chest for that purpose. Now you know how I figured he was out of their *calabozo*. If Morg can stand up and straddle a horse, his mind works . . . Are you sure there was a fight down there, in Messico?"

"An ambush by the Mexicans," said Jeff

with some quiet, malicious, satisfaction; guerrillas viewed it as almost unpardonable to be caught in ambushes. This was *their* sport; without exception they did this to *others,* others never did it to *them.*

But Will Ray Scarbrough simply spat out his smoke, stepped on it and made only an oblique allusion to the ambush. "How many of Morg's men got hurt?"

Jeff only knew how many had survived. He did not know how many men Morgan Scarbrough had had with him, so he said, "There are four men and your brother left."

Will Ray grunted, which could have been his reaction to surprise, chagrin, or even perhaps disgust. With Will Ray it was hard to tell.

Hyatt returned, slightly breathless, and said, "That damned Henry's went and disappeared."

Jeff explained. "I sent him off. Don't

worry about it." With the other two watching, Jeff then drew out his watch, consulting it for the second time within the past half hour. Without explaining, as he returned the watch to his pocket and motioned for Will Ray to stand up, he said, "Damn-nation; isn't that stage *ever* on time!" He looked over at Marshal Sumner. "My horse is out front, Hyatt. If you'll take Will Ray out back and put him on the horse, I'll ride around and get him."

Outside, along the front roadway, Duro was quiet in the bland night. There was a thin, wailing sound of someone playing a fiddle up at Murphy's saloon, otherwise the town was somnolent-seeming. Jeff smoked, wondering whether this was a legitimate feeling, or whether the town, somehow or other, knew or perhaps only suspected, what might be afoot, and was sitting back holding its breath concerning the outcome.

Well; one way or another, he was committed.

Across the road there were two lamps burning in the general store. He thought of Joyce, of how very close he had come to touching her in the barn today, then he put that out of his mind, walked out, untied the seal-brown, stepped up across leather, wheeled right and walked up the road to an intersection with the east-west roadway. He turned left as far as the entrance to the alleyway, rode slowly down it with his head cocked, listening. What he wanted so much to hear, did not materialise. He swore under his breath, went on down, took the led-horse from Hyatt, and when the marshal muttered, "Good luck," Jeff just nodded, then turned and rode slowly back up in the direction of his own barn-lot.

He halted once, where there was sufficient light for him to consult his watch again. Will Ray, who had seen him do this twice now, scowled.

"What the hell you doing, figuring out some kind of timetable?"

Jeff pocketed the watch without replying and went almost up to the entrance to his own back-lot. There, he halted, placed both hands atop the saddlehorn and sat bleakly waiting.

Will Ray looked puzzled, but having been rebuffed once by silence, he did not say anything. They sat for almost ten full minutes before Jeff heard what he'd been waiting with increasing exasperation to hear—the rattle and clanking of the south-bound stage coming down out of the night towards the upper end of town.

Then he eased his horse ahead, tugged at the led-horse and rode on into his barn lot.

FIFTEEN

THE GETAWAY

Henry was out there, invisible to the pair of mounted men, but he had been faithful to his orders. Jeff heard the horses go snorting in a loose run out the back of his faggot-corral. Will Ray heard them scattering across the night-time desert too, and sat his saddle looking baffled.

Behind them, the coach rattled into town, leather-faced wheel-brakes hissing, chain tugs rattling slack as the vehicle slowed out front of the way-station.

Jeff sat impassively waiting. When Henry appeared, mounted and ready, Jeff did no more than glance in his direction, then he lifted his rein-hand and led off almost due northward. The stage had come in heading south. It would depart in that same direction. The loose horses were running southwesterly, and, presumably, they would eventually bend around to also travel southward, which was the only direction they would feel at home in, this far north of Mexico.

Jeff said nothing as he booted the seal-brown over into a slow lope. Henry, on the far side of Will Ray, did the same, so Will Ray's led-horse followed those two examples. They did not slacken pace for a full two miles, and then, instead of settling to a walk, Jeff led on at a stiff trot for another mile and a half. Then, finally, he hauled down, stopped, sat perfectly still for a while, listening, and when he lifted his rein-hand again, Will Ray said, "Ain't you clever though?"

Jeff did not respond.

They began a large half-circle that cut high and around, and eventually southward, but not to their right, which would

have been easterly and eventually southward, but rather almost due west, for a distance, before they descended southward
down in the direction of the border. Of
course Jeff would ultimately have to swing
southeastward because Nogales was down
there, but his calculations included the
notion that Morgan Scarbrough would,
hopefully, divide his men, sending at least
two of them after the loose-stock, which
was supposed to suggest that Will Ray was
being borne away by a hard-riding posse,
and Morgan himself—possibly—and his
remaining two men, would go after the
stage, which by now would already be on
its way southward from Duro.

Jeff would have preferred having at least
two more tricks up his sleeve, to complete
the bafflement of the outlaws, but he had
decided against that on the grounds that in
order to set up any more ruses he would
have had to have taken another three or

four men into his confidence, which was something he shrank from doing. His undertaking was risky enough without increasing that factor.

But nothing happened. They made good time. Henry was silent until they had put about six miles behind them, which may have been some kind of record for Henry, who was usually garrulous under almost any circumstances, but when they passed an old, crumbly mud square, which Jeff had seen many times before without paying much heed, Henry pointed and said, "If we get lucky tonight we'll make out like them fellers did, back thirty years."

The implication was clear—there had been men forted up in that old ruin one time—but neither Jeff nor Will Ray even looked over, something which did not deter old Henry in the slightest.

"Was eleven of 'em," he recounted. "Nine soljers and a 'breed scout, a feller named Garrison, and me. Me'n Garrison quartered around until the bronco-bucks caught our sign, then we high-tailed it down here. Them lousy Apaches come streaking it right along in front of the old adobe. Those boys inside opened up and when it was over me'n Garrison and the 'breed collected four horses each, a mess of guns, and the soljers took three hurt prisoners."

Scarbrough looked back at the rain-washed adobe ruin, looked at Henry, and said, "You should've stayed with fightin' In'ians, old-timer. How are you at praying?"

Henry snorted. "If there's a feller out here tonight that'd better be prayin', mister it's not me."

They completed their southward leg just as Scarbrough, seemingly with dawning anxieties that Jeff Stuart might have in mind delivering him over the line to the

Mexicans, said, "Where in hell you taking me, Stuart?"

Jeff did not answer. They changed course, skirting southeastward now, but gradually coming into a more easterly direction, and Will Ray, apparently relieved, relaxed in the saddle. He could move his manacled hands only high enough to reach the saddlehorn, but no higher.

Jeff kept alert, even though, as Hyatt Sumner had said, once they got clear of town, Jeff would be safer on the desert than almost anyone among the outlaws who might be looking for him, even if Morgan Scarbrough had recruited some desert-raised *peon* from Mex-town.

They had been out almost three hours when Will Ray asked for water. They had to halt in order that Henry could hold up the canteen for the manacled prisoner to drink. Afterwards, instead of thanking the gunsmith, Scarbrough said, "Now a smoke."

Jeff smiled and shook his head. "A good try, but no luck."

Scarbrough sneered. "Ain't no one down here to see it."

Jeff agreed. "Probably not. I sure hope there isn't. But a man can *smell* it two miles on a night like this."

They kept moving. There was nothing out there with them, no Swift foxes, no wild horses. The moon rode high, the stars were serenely indifferent to whatever involvements men far below got themselves into, and the spring-scent of blooming creosote-bush, paloverdes, sage and thornpin bushes made the pleasantly warm night air fragrant in a distinctly unique manner. Only the desert smelt acrid and pleasant at the same time, and it only did it in springtime; the rest of the year it had an odour that put most men in mind of brimstone, ancient dust and ancient, open graves.

Scarbrough finally said, "What a hell of a country," in an almost conversational tone of voice, as he looked left and right.

Jeff responded, his earlier and prevailing mood of watchfulness subsiding a little, now that so much time and so many miles had passed behind their horses. "I have to agree with you."

Scarbrough seized upon this opening, stared hard at Jeff and said, "Then what in the hell are you doing down here?"

Jeff answered enigmatically. "I like it. That's not why I originally came down here, but that was a long time back, when I was a young buck. Now, well, I've got to sort of like it. One thing; you never suffer from frostbite."

Henry laughed softly. "That's a plumb fact. You never suffer from frostbite."

Scarbrough ignored the gunsmith and kept staring hard at Jeff. "I got to thinking last night, Stuart . . . You'd ought to talk to Morg."

Jeff's comment to that suggestion was dry. "No, I don't think so."

Will Ray did not give up. "What in hell's it got you, hidin' out down here cringin' like a cur dog waitin' for a bunch of pot-bellied Yankees back in Washington to say you can live like a human bein' again? Morg told me years back, he wouldn't bow his head to no man, let alone a passel of blue-bellied bastards."

Henry Steele bristled. "You'd better shut your mouth, Scarbrough."

The outlaw cast only a sidelong glance at Henry, then went to work on Jeff again. "Morg'd sure take to you, Stuart. You're smart enough to fit right in. And we live good."

"Yeah," said Henry sarcastically, "it sure looks like you do. Got your damned hands in chains, on your way to be sentenced to prison—if they don't stand you against a brick wall. Yeah, you fellers sure do live good."

Scarbrough's long, thin mouth curled with deep scorn. "Oh, shut up, you old bastard," he growled.

Out of nowhere Steele's right fist appeared, moving in a silvery blur with a wide, long knifeblade vivid in the watery night-light.

Scarbrough recoiled, leaning far to his left in the saddle and Jeff snapped at the gunsmith. "Put that damned thing away, Henry. That's enough from both of you. Keep quiet and just ride. *Henry,* I said put that gawddamned thing away!"

Steele's wiry, thin arm was poised for the final thrust. Anyone seeing the look on his face would not have doubted but that he meant to kill Will Ray Scarbrough; certainly Scarbrough did not seem to doubt it. He sat over so far he was in actual danger of falling off his horse. Even when Henry reluctantly pulled the big blade back, Will Ray still watched it.

The interlude passed. They rode along in silence for another mile, then Henry hissed and raised a hand, pointing north-ward. Jeff had heard nothing, and because of the brush, which was thickest the closer one rode to the easterly border, over in the generally southward direction of Nogales, the less opportunity there was for anyone to see anything, either. But Jeff drew rein, swung down without a sound, stepped ahead between his horse and Scarbrough's mount, where he could instantly clamp a hand hard over soft nostrils if either animal sought to nicker, and waited.

Across from him Henry was at the head of his mount too. He leaned and whis-pered. "Heard it plain as day up there. Shod horse scuffing through chat."

Will Ray, sitting perfectly erect atop his

animal, strained in the direction Henry had indicated. He had more reason than either of his companions to hope with all his strength there might be someone up there. This late at night and this far from either Nogales or Duro, it wouldn't be anyone with a very legitimate reason for night-riding. Even if it wasn't Will Ray's brother and the other outlaws, that would be all right too.

Jeff had almost abandoned the idea that there might be someone northeast of them, when they all heard the sound, this second time. It was, as Henry had said, a shod horse rattling over small stones, and it seemed to be perhaps no more than a quarter or a half mile above them. Actual distances were impossible to estimate in the night-time on the desert, even for men like old Henry Steele, and Jeff Stuart, who were experienced.

Jeff thought it was three riders, but that

could have been far wrong too. The only thing he and Henry could be fairly certain of, was that there was more than *one* rider up there.

Will Ray shifted in his saddle. Jeff felt the horse alter stance to compensate, and turned to look up. "Remember what I told you back in town," he whispered.

Will Ray glanced downward, bitterly; he remembered, evidently, because he did not make another move nor act as though he might make a sound.

The riders faded out. Jeff thought they were riding southward. He knew for a fact that the stageroad was several miles northward, and about parallel to the route of the invisible horsemen. As he turned back to mount his horse he decided to drop down southward another couple of miles, so that those strangers up there would not hear *him*, as he had heard them, then to resume his direct bearing towards Nogales.

Will Ray glowered as soon as they changed course. He probably would have said something aloud, or at least have cursed a little, since he knew exactly why they had changed course, but the bland, steady gaze he got from Jeff kept him silent.

Henry waited a long time, almost until they were ready to swing eastward again, before speaking. "That'd be them," he told Jeff. "Either the bunch that ride after the coach, or them as went off after your loose horses—who probably cut around southward down here. Jeff; be a hell of a note if we was *between* 'em, wouldn't it?"

Jeff said nothing. He had considered the full route before ever riding out of Duro, and, unlike Hyatt Sumner, who had feared Jeff would not be able to get clear of Duro, Jeff's worries had never really centred around Duro at all. His worries had centred around the country north and west of

Nogales.

Will Ray's brother would know that unless he found his brother on the stage, or somewhere else upon the desert, his best chance of intercepting him would be down around Nogales, which was the obvious destination of the men taking his brother away from Duro. *That* country, then, down near the border town, would be where the real danger lay.

Jeff had an ace up his sleeve about that, too, but he did not confide it in his companion now, any more than he had confided in Hyatt Sumner back at Duro.

SIXTEEN

THE NIGHT FLIGHT

When Jeff finally figured out that despite all his precautions, all his foresight and wariness, he actually was not a match for Morgan Scarbrough, the renegade former Confederate guerrilla commander, was when they were still about fifteen miles—twelve at the least—from Nogales, down where the country began to thin out slightly, as though generations of Mex faggot-gatherers had industriously plied their trade through the thickets, and where there was more scattered, open country.

Down there, he heard the riders before Henry did, hauled up, swung down and stepped to his horse's head again. This time old Henry had heard nothing, and even though he emulated Jeff, he leaned and said, "Didn't notice nothing."

Jeff replied quietly. "You were right, back there five miles, Henry. They're behind us—and in front too."

Steele gave a slight start, and twisted to look back. "You sure, Jeff; I didn't hear a thing."

Will Ray looked down, wolfishly smiling at the old man. Will Ray had not forgot that interlude with the big-bladed old Bowie knife.

Jeff's answer was calm. "You're never sure in the dark, but I smelled tobacco smoke and it's coming from up yonder. Behind us, a horse blew its nose a long way back."

"Don't have to be them," suggested Henry, with more prayerful hope than conviction.

Jeff did not respond to that for a while, and even when he spoke again, he did not respond to it, he said, simply, "They're not moving, up ahead, Henry. Here; mind my horse, I'm going out and have a look."

"Gawddammit, boy, be careful." Henry took the seal-brown's reins, and for the first time got an expression of genuine worry upon his face. What made it worse for the gunsmith was that he had heard nothing. He still heard nothing. Actually, the faint sounds that Jeff had detected did not necessarily have to be what he thought they were, but he had been riding for a number of hours now, with an acute wariness; it had made him critically responsive to anything which fitted into a pattern of thought relevant to what now gripped his entire awareness. He *knew,* with nothing more substantive than instinct, that he was being tracked down by Morgan Scarbrough, the seasoned, successful guerrilla commander.

As he went ahead through the night, soundlessly, and pulled free the little leather thong which held his belt-gun in place, he was certain that his chance of reaching Nogales with Will Ray Scarbrough was slipping away minute by minute. He had no proof of it at all, but he *knew* it.

A man's voice, softly borne out of the onward distance, came indistinctly. If there had been a slurred Texas accent, that too had not survived the distance. But Jeff stopped dead-still and waited. There was no second voice-sound, though, so he walked ahead, much more slowly from here on.

It was not hard to guess how the men behind them had come up, back there. They had eventually discovered that they were chasing loose horses. Maybe they had discovered it back closer to Duro; experienced horsemen would know the difference after no more than about a mile, providing they could get that close, and apparently the renegades *had* got that close, and had then probably followed an earlier order to head at once down in the direction of Nogales.

Jeff stepped forth from a thicket, saw a mounted man dead ahead as a skylined, high silhouette, and froze with the brush at his back, preventing the horseman from detecting him.

He could make nothing out, actually, except that that was a mounted man ahead and far across an open place, but from the shadow's erect bearing, from his obvious posture of watching, waiting, and listening, Jeff did not have to see more. He waited, wishing the horseman would turn back. When that did not occur, Jeff finally inched back deeper through the underbrush, then hastened all the way back where Henry was waiting.

He grabbed his reins, mounted, pointed southward and led off without speaking.

Henry got the desperate implication, evidently, because he kept silent and brought Will Ray's horse along, keeping tight hold of the lead-shank instead of giving it back to Jeff.

They had a lot of country between them and the border. In fact, providing they did not go back northward again, there was entirely too much country down there for anyone to find them, by accident. If they were detected, it would have to be the result of something better than just sheer luck.

Eventually, when he thought they had covered enough ground, Jeff explained what he had encountered. Will Ray nodded sagely. "That's only the beginning," he assured them. "You can't out-guess Morgan. No one can."

That irritated Jeff, but he kept this feeling to himself. He had his private and personal feelings on this, and he was willing to concede—to himself—that Morgan Scarbrough had done a masterful job, considering that he only had four men and hundreds of miles in the desert, at night, to do it in. But Jeff still had an ace up his sleeve.

They finally got within perhaps twenty miles of the border before angling eastward again. This time, although Jeff made no mention of it, he had no intention of altering course again. Nor did he.

Henry began to recover some of his earlier assurance, now. When he felt that they had passed well beyond that area, up north, where the horseman had been waiting, he looked over at Will Ray with a bitter smile and said, "No one's ever outguessed your brother? You remember that, come dawn. I'd like to hear you say it then."

Scarbrough may have felt too much scorn to reply, or he may have also begun to have some second thoughts; in either case he simply stared at the gunsmith, then slowly turned back to watching the onward land.

The night was beginning to turn slightly chilly. It only did this on the far desert when the hour was up close to midnight, or later. Jeff did not look at his watch. The time would be important to them only when it got closer to sunrise. If they hadn't made it to Nogales by then . . . Jeff slouched along, ticking off the probable miles in his head. He was just beginning to think they might make it, when someone riding a horse hard, came southward heading down across their route.

It happened so suddenly, so unexpectedly, that Henry fumbled for his gun and began to curse, as though they were under personal attack. But that by itself would probably have caused them no trouble. It was Hyatt Sumner's horse, upon which

Will Ray Scarbrough was riding, that insured the arrival of trouble. He threw up his head before any of them could prevent it, and nickered ahead at that invisible running horse. Without any warning the racing rider up ahead twisted in his saddle, and fired. The blast of red-orange light startled them all. The gunthunder was deafening. Old Henry let off a squawk. He had his gun out and rising, and although he swung his horse sidewards as though to shoot back, he did not do it.

Will Ray gasped and ducked low. Jeff, with both hands occupied, could not loop the lead-shank quickly enough to get his gun, not *that* time, but he made the hard-and-fast loop afterwards.

Below, where that racing rider was going, or at least in the due-southward direction he seemed to be riding, someone else let fly with a gunshot. This one was some distance away. Jeff could neither see the flame nor fix the place where the weapon had been fired. He did not get much of a chance, because a third gunman cut loose, but this one was on Jeff's left, in the direction the fleeing man had come.

They drew rein quickly. Henry Steele and Jeff Stuart, with fidgeting Will Ray Scarbrough between them. A rider, evidently racing in the wake of that first man, but swerving more inland on *his* flight, suddenly loomed so close Jeff very distinctly saw the look on the man's face—then the man's gunhand swung. Henry fired first. The horseman pinwheeled, his astonished mount raced ahead, stirrups flopping, and Will Ray cried out a name.

"Bowie! Bowie!"

After Henry's shot, there was a long moment of shocked silence. It seemed to Jeff as though whoever was out there, evidently ahead, northward and southward of him, had been as astonished to have someone fire a gun where Henry Steele was sitting, as Henry and Jeff had originally been when that racing horseman had sped in front of them.

Jeff called to Henry to dismount. He reached to catch Will Ray's attention too, but Will Ray was still staring where that thrown-man was lying flat out on his back.

Jeff stepped down, moved round where Will Ray was, reached high and gave a powerful wrench. Will Ray came to earth. On the opposite side of Will Ray's horse Henry Steele had stepped to earth also, but Henry had now put up his sixgun and had tugged out his Winchester.

The man over there on his back, moaned. Jeff pushed Will Ray ahead for a shield, and with Henry watching their prisoner, Jeff knelt beside the downed man. Henry's bullet had pinwheeled that outlaw off his horse by grazing up alongside the man's face at the cheekbone, and angling upwards past his temple, into his hair, and stunning him. Jeff reached, flung the man's gun away, pushed his own gun into the man's face, then helped the man sit up.

Whoever Bowie was, the moment he opened his mouth and demonstrated that whiny, nasal drawl of Texas, Jeff knew they had another prisoner. Bowie stared dumbly at Jeff, then at Henry, and finally at Will Ray. Finally, then, his eyes showed a flicker in the starshine. He started to speak, to say, "Don't worry none, Will Ray," when a sudden violent flurry of gunfire erupted. Bullets clipped underbrush on all sides. Bowie suddenly gave a great start, as though to spring to his feet, then he fell forward and struck Henry in the legs, nearly upsetting him. One of those stray bullets had caught Bowie above the eyes in the forehead.

Jeff yelled at old Henry, but he was already kicking free to drop flat. Will Ray went down too, but he bawled out.

"Over here, Morg, *over here!*"

Neither Jeff nor Henry had a chance to do anything about that; gunshots boring straight in from slightly to the northwest, clipped tiny, leathery thornpin leaves making all three men go perfectly flat until the initial fusillade was finished. Then old Henry pushed out his Winchester, snugged it back, and waited.

Jeff could not figure it all out. Two things seemed certain, and for the moment he was content to concentrate entirely upon them. The first thing was that Morgan was out there. The second thing was that, so were a lot of other people with guns.

Henry suddenly raised his head from over the rear sight and said, in a voice of almost adolescent astonishment, "Well, I'll be gawddamned, Jeff—them's *soljers!*"

Jeff had no time to look all around. A

stealthily-moving large man, a gun in each hand, came out of the onward underbrush peering over his shoulder. He faced suddenly forward, responding probably to instinct because he could not see the prone men.

Will Ray gasped and raised up stiffly. Henry reached, clubbed Will Ray flat, and the oncoming man heard that. Jeff saw his right-hand gun moving—and called to him.

"Drop it!"

The large man, instead of obeying, was sufficiently distracted by the voice from a different direction, that he fired prematurely, the bullet caused an explosion of sand and fine gravel in Will Ray's face, then two guns exploded simultaneously. Jeff fired his Colt and Henry tugged off a round from his Winchester.

The big man went backward, knocked there by the mule-kick impact of those two bullets. He fell into a spidery, resilient large bush, and hung there as though impaled.

A scattered rattle of more distant, southerly, gunfire broke out. It only lasted a moment or two, then someone shouted from due west.

"Hey; you up ahead of us. If you're from Duro fire off two rounds fast!"

Jeff tipped his Colt, snapped off two fast shots, then lowered the gun, rolled to one side and began quickly to kick out the spent casings so that he could plug in fresh loads from his shellbelt.

"Army!" That same bull-bass voice sang out. "Hold your damned fire!"

Will Ray was digging at both eyes with his fists when the line of troopers emerged, over near where that dead man still hung in the underbrush like a huge, broken spider.

Old Henry let off a warwhoop and got stiffly up to his feet. He waved his carbine as the soldiers clustered close to the bush, staring at the dead man. One of them spoke, not loudly at all, but Jeff heard him without straining.

"By gawd, they got Morgan!"

SEVENTEEN

THE HOMING INSTINCT

The army took Will Ray into custody. He sat like stone, still manacled but slumped now, watching them lash his dead brother belly-down across a horse.

One outlaw had escaped. The man who had initially fled southward, apparently abandoning Morgan Scarbrough and the other three; the same racing horseman who had passed down-country in front of Jeff and Henry, and who had first fired at them, was not found, and the soldier-patrol did not go look for him.

The other three men, including the one Will Ray had called Bowie, were dead. As the lieutenant in charge of the patrol stood aside with Jeff and explained, his troopers did what had to be done with the prisoner and the corpses.

The army had been alerted by Marshal Sumner's plea for help, and had sent forth three patrols. One patrol had gone up the road straight for Duro; the purpose for this, said the lieutenant, was to lend support to the stage coach if the outlaws tried to stop it looking for Will Ray. The second patrol had made a big sashay northwesterly, hoping to intercept the outlaws up in the vicinity of Duro.

The third patrol, according to the lieutenant, who ironically smiled as he explained, had taken the more southerly stretch of country, on the off-chance the outlaws might try to make a run for Mexico again.

"We thought it would be purely routine," stated the officer, who was a leathery individual, older-looking than most junior-grade officers Jeff had known years back. "I had scouts out, as usual. They damned near bumped into a mounted man who seemed to be trying to pick up some sign south of the stageroad. We struck out, then, spooked 'em, and they came southward. But hell, I had no inkling at all you men would be this far dow-country."

Jeff said, "Damned wonder didn't the lot of us all get killed, the way that shootin' was going on."

A sergeant came over, a grizzled, pug-nosed man with reddish hair and small, close-set pale eyes. He told the officer they were ready to head back for Nogales. The lieutenant nodded at the sergeant, then turned and smiled at Jeff and Henry. "As confusing as the whole damned mess was, you boys accomplished one thing in the darkness that'll go down in the history books; you wrote *finis* to the outlaw career of the last of the oldtime Rebel guerilla leaders."

He nodded briskly and leaned to tug his

gauntlets on. "I'll see that a receipt for Will Ray is sent to the U.S. deputy marshal up at Duro. Good-night, gentlemen."

Jeff nodded slowly, and watched as the troopers mounted and reined off back through the night, in the general direction of Nogales. Finally, he let all his breath out in a rattling sigh and shifted stance, pushed his hat back and looked soberly at Henry Steele. Without speaking he rolled a cigarette, lit it, and gazed at the big bush where Morgan Scarbrough had died.

"Damndest night I ever put in," he said, eventually, keeping his voice low and soft.

Henry was reloading as he replied to that. "I've put in a few that was just as bad . . . by the way, Jeff, which bullet you reckon finished off Morgan Scarbrough?"

Jeff shrugged out of his reverie as he started back towards their horses. "Yours," he said. "Let's get the hell back to town. If we push a little we might be able to make it before sunup."

That was a wishful thought. Jeff knew just how wishful after an hour of riding calmly, reflectively, and for the first time he knew how much ground they really had covered.

They were still heading north when the sun arrived. Three hours later, when the heat was building up, they were also still riding. Old Henry passed over the canteen, took it back, emptied it into himself, draped it from the horn, squinted around and said, "You really figure it was my carbine slug killed Morgan Scarbrough?"

Jeff woodenly nodded. "I'm plumb sure."

"Will you say that to Hyatt?"

"Yeah."

Jeff finally saw Duro, shimmery and falsely bright, far ahead. His personal, inner feeling was that he would have gladly exchanged any claim he might have had on the Scarbrough reward, for this one sighting. Not because he was so enthralled by the town; there was another newer and fresher reason for his feeling.

They did not actually reach Duro until mid-afternoon. It was tantalising to ride all of the late morning towards a clearly visible goal, and have that goal continually recede from them.

They went directly to the back-alley horse-shed out back of Hyatt Sumner's office, and put up the borrowed horse, fed him, saw to it that he could get to the water-trough, then banged on the rear office door and when Hyatt came out, blinking his surprise, Henry spoke before Jeff could even get his mouth open.

"I got him, Hyatt. I got Morgan Scarbrough with m' carbine. Ask Jeff, he'll confirm it. Now, I was wondering—how does a man go about collecting the reward?"

Marshal Sumner said nothing for a

moment. He listened to Henry, then he raised his eyes to Jeff. "What happened; where's Will Ray?"

"Army took him over on the south desert, where they also lashed three dead men, including Morgan, across some horses, and headed back for Nogales," replied Jeff. "Hyatt, Henry'll tell you all about it. Right now, I'm going up home and put up my horse, get a drink of well-water and something to eat . . . And—that's right, Henry got Morgan."

Jeff turned and—strode away northward up the alleyway leading his tired seal-brown. Hyatt seemed upon the verge of calling him back, but he didn't do it, which was probably just as well, because Jeff would not have heard him.

The heat was fully up, now, and the springtime day was hot even in the shade. When Jeff crossed the yard towards his barn, though, he was not the slightest bit aware of heat, or tiredness, or thirst, or anything else.

Joyce was in the golden-lighted corral with her sorrel horse. She had heard him coming, and was standing over there, very stiff, watching as he came into sight.

She ran to the corral gate, closed it after herself and ran into the barn where he had gone, and where he was now waiting.

He raised his arms to her. She responded as though this was something they had done many times before. She did not hang back, nor even momentarily hesitate, but pressed hard against him full length, cool, soft arms up around his shoulders.

The kiss was violent for them both, and afterwards, when she pulled away and buried her face against him, she said, "I told the sorrel horse that was what I was going to do when you came back."

Jeff smiled. "What did he think of the

idea?"

"Oh; he favoured it," she replied, giggling, still with her face hidden. "In fact he was the one who told me you were coming."

Jeff closed his arms round her, dropped his face a little, caught that sweet, soap-scent, and soundlessly sighed. *This* made all the rest of it worthwhile.

Center Point Publishing
600 Brooks Road ● PO Box 1
Thorndike ME 04986-0001 USA

(207) 568-3717

US & Canada:
1 800 929-9108